HOUSE OF HOLLY

Also by MARJORIE MUELLER FREER

GAY ENTERPRISES (about baking and cooking)
SHOWCASE FOR DIANE (about display work)
ROBERTA, INTERIOR DECORATOR

HOUSE
OF HOLLY

By Marjorie Mueller Freer

J 787772

JULIAN MESSNER, INC. · NEW YORK

Published by Julian Messner, Inc.
8 West 40th Street, New York 18
Published Simultaneously in Canada
By The Copp Clark Company, Limited

Second Printing, February, 1955

Library of Congress Catalog Card No. 54-10584

This story of many threads is dedicated to many people

—to Aunt Rose, Mother and Dad,
Gretchen Clapp, Ring Carde, Dorothy
Freer Fernee and Elizabeth Scott; to
my brothers, Walter and Bob; and to
Bonnie, Penny and Howe who live
with my bookmaking.

HOUSE OF HOLLY

About the Author

MARJORIE MUELLER FREER writes of mail order from personal experience. For the past seven years she has been conducting Practical Playwriting, a correspondence course featuring the writing of stage, radio and television plays. Her students-by-mail are located all over the United States and Canada. Like her heroine Holly, Mrs. Freer, who is a graduate of Barnard College and has done graduate work in drama and stage design at Columbia University, feels that one of the exciting things about a mail-order business is that you never know what you are going to take out of your mailbox. Along with assignments to correct, inquiries and registrations, she has received surprise packages from students, including a bouquet of trailing arbutus from New Hampshire and a huge box of assorted Christmas greens from California. Correspondence students, Mrs. Freer adds, tell you in detail about themselves, and they want to know about you and your family too.

Marjorie Freer's hobbies are many and again, like Holly, she likes to be a "designing woman," creating original costume and home accessories and dolls. In addition to her career novels, she has written a how-to book of original gifts, sold hat designs to a national magazine, and has a standing order in several gift shops for the golden tree which figures in HOUSE OF HOLLY.

To get the "feel" of the Housatonic Valley of Connecticut, which is the background of her new book, Mrs. Freer and her family, which includes her husband, the artist, Howard Freer, and their daughters, Bonnie and Penny, spent a year and a half commuting to Oxford, Woodbury and Southbury. Azalea Acres was inspired by an estate which belongs to friends of the Freers, and the benefit garden party described in the book actually took place. *The Goodhill Gazette* was also inspired by an actual mimeographed newspaper, *The Acorn Journal*, published and edited by a ten-year-old friend of the Freer girls. And for firsthand experience in a phase of mail order undertaken by Holly, the author and a close friend created doll and accessory patterns which they sold via the R.F.D. Although they stopped the ads four months ago, orders are still coming in.

CHAPTER

1

Marooned. Marooned for the summer miles from anywhere. Holly Elliot drew an exasperated breath and continued along the country road. This afternoon there wasn't even a sound to break the monotony. No scream of a sea gull. No surf swishing against the shore. No reassuring roar of an outboard motor. None of the familiar salt-water sounds and sights and smells that had made up the pattern of school vacations as long as she could remember—just fields and woods and hills and occasional houses. And why? Just because her family had been offered a free rent for the summer.

Substituting the Housatonic Valley of Connecticut for the coast of Maine had been bad enough. What made it worse was that there was absolutely no one around here her own age—no teen-agers at all, as far as she had been able to discover. Oh, yes, plenty of small fry who had materialized out of nowhere for her ten-year-old brother, Hugh, and her eight-year-old brother, Roy, to pal around with. Adults, too, for whenever her parents felt the need of sociability. But for her there was no one.

Right this moment, she knew, the teen crowd at Christmas Cove would be having a wonderful time. Perhaps they were

[1]

off on a clambake, or out fishing for flounder or sailing, or swimming or riding somewhere in a jeep. Whatever they were doing, it would be fun . . . something she was being short-changed on. You'd think parents would show a little under-standing, but hers had been so intent on her father's change of jobs that she had somehow been lost in the shuffle. It wouldn't have been quite so bad if they had stayed on until fall in New London, where both her mother and her father had taught at the junior college this past year. At least there would have been a summer full of fun with the old crowd. Here there was nothing to do except walk, and that wasn't very interesting when you had to go by yourself. She didn't even feel like doing anything in the needlework or craft line —both favorite occupations with which she had done nothing for some time.

Just ahead, a side road branched off from the one she was on. Should she turn back or keep on? All the roads seemed to lead endlessly up and down over the hills in all directions, but this turn to the left was one she hadn't been on. Behind her sounded the ungainly rumble of a truck. Holly stepped aside for it to pass; but the vehicle continued straight ahead, clat-tered off into silence. Now, by contrast, it was even quieter than before.

Walking down the new road and taking note of her sur-roundings, she was surprised to see a number of small houses, bright with new paint and with a summer-resortish air, built closer together than any other places she had seen around here. But for all the signs of life from them, this might have been a ghost settlement. Soon there were no more buildings —only trees pressing in from either side. Then a sound obtruded. At first she thought she was only willing herself to hear it; but, where it had been faint at first, it grew louder and louder, then abruptly was cut off. Her footsteps quickened—it had been an outboard motor and somewhere up ahead must be water. Half running, she saw sandbanks to her left and then on the right a cove carved deeply into the land. Tied to the trees on the bank were quite a number of rowboats; and even as she watched, another dinghy, with outboard motor uptilted, glided in. This must have been what she had heard. A sun-bronzed boy—he couldn't be too much older than her own seventeen—was the only occupant.

"Hi!" he hailed her with a cheery grin.

"Hi!" Holly returned his greeting. "I didn't realize there was water this close."

He nodded. "Lake Zoar. Part of the Housatonic River." Then, looking up from his work of making fast the boat, "You must be new here."

Holly felt herself smiling. "Yes." And as she noted his fishing rod and pail, "Any luck?"

"Pretty fair. Enough for a meal." Picking up his gear, he stood up and, even though she was above him on the bank, she could see how tall he was.

"Want me to take the rod?"

"Okay—thanks." A moment later he leaped ashore, stood towering above her. "My name's Mark Logan," he offered.

"I'm Holly Elliot."

"Holly." He smiled down at her companionably. "Do you live around here?"

"Up at Professor Roberts'."

"Then we're practically neighbors."

[3]

Holly looked her surprise.

"I'm helping out at Azalea Acres during college vacation." he explained.

"Where's that?"

"The pink house around the corner and up the hill from here. Used to belong to a famous opera singer. There's just one other place between the Fairchilds' and the Roberts'. But I didn't know the professor and his family were back," he added. "Mrs. Fairchild said he was down in the Southwest somewhere doing work on a fellowship."

"He still is. But my father and he are friends; so when he heard Dad was going to teach at the Taft School in Watertown this fall, he asked us if we'd stay at his place and look after things while we were house hunting."

"Who's us?" Mark wanted to know.

"Mother, Dad, and my two brothers. Hugh's ten and Roy's eight."

"A wonder they haven't been over."

"Don't worry. They will be. And when they do come"— Holly couldn't suppress a mischievous smile—"watch out!"

"Characters?"

"That's one way of putting it."

"Don't worry. I'll whittle them down to size."

She looked up at him, consciously noting for the first time the gray blue of his eyes, his wavy shock of wheat-colored hair. "Maybe."

"You doubt me?"

Taking in the rather determined set of his chin, Holly chuckled. "You just don't know my brothers!"

Mark was back in the dinghy again, unscrewing the out-

[4]

board motor. "To me there's just one important thing about Hugh and Roy."

"What's that?"

"They have a sister."

Holly was enjoying this. "Oh?"

His eyes were on her. "She's a girl I'd like to get to know."

Holly decided that this was as good an exit cue as any. "It's been nice meeting you," she told Mark, and headed up the path toward the road.

"Where are you going?"

"Home."

"Wait a minute!" He lifted the engine ashore, placed it carefully on its side. "Don't you want a lift? Mrs. Fairchild is coming down to pick me up."

"Well . . ." Holly hesitated. It was hard to know what to do. She didn't want the meeting to come to an end and yet she didn't wish to appear overanxious.

"You'll get home much quicker that way," he urged, checking with his wrist watch. "Mrs. Fairchild said she'd be here around five and it's almost that now."

"I wouldn't want to impose on her."

He laughed. "Impose? If you knew her, you wouldn't say that. She's the original human dynamo and she just loves to do things for people. You might almost say people are her hobby—people and gardens," he added.

Still wondering what to do, Holly glanced up as she detected the approaching purr of a car which turned out to be an expensively elegant station wagon.

"That's Mrs. Fairchild now," Mark informed her.

The auburn-haired woman at the wheel backed the car around, then got out to join them.

"Look what I just fished out of the lake," Mark announced, indicating Holly.

"Mark, you're impossible!" she laughed, then turned her warm regard on Holly. "Don't ever pay any attention to anything he says."

Holly smiled. "Mrs. Fairchild, I'm Holly Elliot."

"I'm glad to know you, Holly." The clasp of her large hand was firm and her gold-flecked brown eyes were filled with friendly interest.

"Holly and her family are living up at the Roberts place," Mark explained.

"How long have you been there?"

"Almost a week."

"That long?" Her voice held dismay. "If I'd known, I would have been up to call! But there's been so much to do lately getting ready for the garden party, I haven't been keeping up on everything I should."

On the way home in the station wagon, seated between Mrs. Fairchild and Mark, Holly couldn't help feeling that the summer was definitely looking up. She felt as though she were floating, and it wasn't just the easy-riding qualities of the car.

Hugh and Roy were playing in the yard but stopped to stare in astonishment as Mark handed her out.

"Thanks for the ride home," she told Mrs. Fairchild, then, with her glance including Mark, added, "Won't you come in to meet Mother and Dad?"

"I'd like to, but it's late and Clem—that's my husband—

will be home any minute. We'll be up before long though, and you and your family must come down to see us. Do you like swimming?"

"I love it."

"We have our own lake. All of you feel free to come down any time."

"Thanks a lot."

Holly was conscious that Mark was looking at her. "See you soon," he promised, and then, as Mrs. Fairchild backed the car out of the drive, he winked as though there were already a secret understanding between them.

Drifting slowly off to sleep that night, Holly hugged the thought of the day to her. Instead of being a place of banishment, Oxford now offered interesting possibilities; and it was a relief to know there was one person in her age group nearby.

In the predawn she awoke to the first cheeps and trills of the birds. Through the windows a cool breeze carried the most delightfully piney and woodsy scent. There was a relaxed, intimate quality to everything this morning, and it was a pleasant part of returning consciousness to know that just a short distance down the road was a boy named Mark. She also couldn't help wondering about the garden party Mrs. Fairchild had mentioned. Was that something to which they would be invited?

With the first hint of sun she dressed in shorts and a halter that brought out the green flecks in her hazel eyes, brushed her new Italian-boy haircut, and went downstairs. Now for the first time she appreciated the entertainment possibilities of the place where they were staying. One ell of the professor's pleasantly rambling fieldstone house was a screened-in outdoor room complete with sturdy picnic table and benches and a huge fireplace at one end. Broom in hand, Holly went out to sweep the cement floor recalling that in one of his letters describing the place to her parents Professor Roberts had said that, once it was heated, the fireplace would remain at baking and roasting temperature for twenty-four hours. It would be fun to cook a meal in it someday soon, and invite Mark up for a picnic-style family meal.

As she worked she was joined by her mother. "What are you doing up so early, Holly?" was her surprised query.

"Oh, I couldn't sleep and, since it is such a nice day, I thought it would be fun to have breakfast out here." She tried to toss it off lightly.

While her mother arranged a bowl of blue forget-me-nots and Johnny-jump-ups—they grew just outside the door—for the centerpiece, Holly set the table. Looking up suddenly at her mother while she was absorbed in fixing the flowers, Holly couldn't help noticing the blue smudges of fatigue under her eyes and the indoor pallor of her skin. She had had a hard bout with the flu last winter and the doctor had suggested that a year away from teaching would be a good idea. Belatedly Holly realized she could have been helping more, instead of wandering about the countryside feeling sorry for herself. On the other hand, if she hadn't happened upon the cove, she might not have met Mark for quite a while or perhaps not at all.

Would he call her today to make some plans, or drop by this evening? After breakfast, with an eye to his coming,

[8]

Holly vacuumed and dusted, rearranged some of the furniture, and gathered bouquets of daisies and other wild flowers.

"Expecting company?" inquired her father on his way to Professor Roberts' study, where he had already started work on the new courses he would teach in the fall. In spite of his preoccupied air, Holly knew only too well from past experience that he was deeply observant of everything that went on around him.

"Not especially," she countered. "But Mrs. Fairchild or someone else might pop in any time, and since Mother's busy catching up on ironing—"

"You and your mother—always worried about what people might think!" he teased.

Next to come in were her brothers—Hugh, shooting up tall and slender and dark like their father; Roy, fair-skinned like their mother and of a rotund, square-riggerish build reminiscent of Grandfather Elliot.

"Whew, but it's hot, Holly! Want to go swimming down at the Fairchilds' lake?" they asked.

Holly was tempted, but going down this afternoon might look as though she were overanxious for another meeting with Mark.

"Can't you see I'm busy?" she told her brothers.

"I bet you made up that story about Mrs. Fairfield inviting us!" exclaimed Hugh, who was a consistent skeptic and needed a lot of convincing.

"Of course I didn't!" she retorted indignantly, then added in a gentler tone, "But why don't you boys go alone?"

Hugh was still not completely sold. "It's probably just a little fishpond."

"Don't be silly!"

"Why don't you go then?"

"I told you—I have things to do."

"Aw, please, Hol."

"I'm sorry. Maybe tomorrow," she half promised.

Her brothers were quick to sense her soft mood. "How about playing some games with us when you're through?"

"All right," she laughingly agreed—and soon found herself trapped in a game of parcheesi, which she considered one of the most stupid pastimes ever invented but which both boys loved. Through three seemingly endless games she found herself listening for the phone.

Mark didn't call before supper. He didn't call or drop by after supper either. Still, Holly told herself as she got ready for bed, it was only twenty-four hours since they had met. But all the following day there was no sign or word from him. If he had lived far away, she could have understood his not coming; but when someone was less than a quarter of a mile distant, it was different. While she didn't want to remember it, Mrs. Fairchild's laughing warning not to believe a word Mark said kept popping into her mind. Still, it was only two days; and he could be busy (but not quite that busy, the practical side of her said) and tomorrow he would surely appear.

The third day there was a visitor from Azalea Acres; but it was Alice Fairchild herself, stopping briefly to meet her parents and to give them a basket of assorted early vegetables from her garden.

By now the boys were so worked up over Holly's continued refusal to go swimming that Roy, who was the bolder of the two, tackled Mrs. Fairchild.

"Didn't you say we could go swimming in your lake?" he demanded.

"I certainly did and we've been looking for you," she smiled. "Why don't you come?"

He turned accusing eyes on Holly. "Sis won't go."

Holly felt indignant at him, and embarrassed too. "I do want to come, Mrs. Fairchild, but I've been busy."

"Not too busy to go swimming, honey," contradicted her father, and Holly gave him an exasperated look. For a man with a Doctor of Philosophy degree, he wasn't smart about some things. But now her mother was explaining to their visitor how hard her daughter had been working to help get the place in order.

"I'm sure she has," Alice Fairchild agreed, then invited them all to come for a dip whenever they felt like it; if the boys were good swimmers, she added, they needn't wait for any of the adults.

"Could we go now?" Roy wanted to know.

"Certainly," she smiled. "Get your trunks and towels and I'll drive you down. You can change in the bathhouse."

When the boys returned, enthusiastic over the size of the lake and the aluminum rowboat which they had also been allowed to use, Holly thought they might volunteer some word about Mark; but, since they said nothing, she decided not to ask.

By the fourth day Holly was both hurt and angry. She wasn't the kind of girl you put in cold storage. As far as she was concerned, she didn't care whether she ever saw Mark

Logan again. What made her even more provoked was the thought that in Christmas Cove one boy would never have loomed so important. Other summers she had always been part of a pack of young people who went everywhere, did everything together. Now she wished she hadn't even met Mark. She had been so happy dreaming of all the fun they'd be having together that now the prospect of a boyless summer was not a very pleasant one.

That afternoon when her father suggested they all go to Watertown with him and look around the town while he had a conference at the school, Holly welcomed the idea. Anything was better than staying around a house where one existed in a vacuum. There wasn't even the prospect of a garden party, for, friendly though she appeared, Alice Fairchild had made no further mention of the event. More than ever Holly found herself wishing that their summer address was anything but Goodhill Road, Oxford, Southbury R. F. D. #2.

CHAPTER

2

The drive to Watertown took them down a long hill and, as they passed Azalea Acres, Holly kept her gaze fixed on the road ahead. But she couldn't miss the fact that someone was running a power mower right outside the white wooden fence.

"There's Mark," Hugh pointed out.

"Hey, Mark!" called Roy, and waved.

"Silly, he can't hear you," Hugh told him.

At mention of Mark, Holly instinctively shrank back into her seat beside her brothers. Funny the boys hadn't said anything about meeting him.

"Who's Mark?" asked their father. "The Fairchilds' son?"

"No. His name is Logan," volunteered Roy.

"He works for the Fairchilds," put in Hugh.

"Only in the summer," supplemented Roy. "The rest of the time he goes to M.I.T." This was news to Holly, but leave it to Roy—one brief meeting with anyone and he usually managed to extract all pertinent facts in the manner of a star reporter.

"Boys, you've been remiss in your duty. How about introducing your sister?" Although her father spoke with a straight face, his eyes, searching her out in the rear-view mirror, were twinkling.

"Holly knows him already," informed Hugh, quite unmindful of her can't-you-ever-mind-your-own-business look.

"Why didn't you tell us, dear?" Her mother's tone was gently reproachful.

"I only met him a few minutes the other day when Mrs. Fairchild brought me home."

"Well, how about turning on a few feminine wiles and luring him up to dinner?" teased her father.

"Oh, Daddy! Please let me alone!"

More than ever she wished she had stayed back at the house. But her mother, at least, sensed she didn't want to talk about him any more; for she called everyone's attention to the lovely old colonial houses that made up the main street of Southbury, through which they were now passing. Next came Woodbury, and what caught Holly's eye even more than the beautiful homes was an artistic circular sign that read THE WAGON WHEEL—GIFTS. The shop was housed in the ell of a charming mansion painted black with white shutters and trim and blooming hollyhocks making a gay pattern of color against the dark background. That was a place she would like to stop in soon. What particularly interested her in establishments like that were the handmades, which often gave her ideas for designs of her own. Sewing, knitting, and crocheting had been high on her list of hobbies ever since she could hold a needle. Though she hadn't done anything in that line for months and months—her last project in the handwork line had been when she showed a Brownie troop how to make rag dolls—she began to feel the desire again. At least she could take up some of the slack this summer by working on her fall and winter wardrobe.

Back in childhood her favorite pastime had always been

playing store, and the idea of working in one still intrigued her. One of these years she wanted to become a fashion buyer and, as one of her older friends who was an accessory buyer had explained, she could work her way up to that from the selling floor. Mother and Dad thought she should go to college first and major in retailing, but she wanted to start right out at a store. Happily for her, she had been given a free hand and she could hardly wait for September.

So deep in thought had Holly been that she hadn't paid much attention to the rolling countryside through which they had been passing. The next thing she knew they had reached the impressive campus of brick buildings that made up Taft. Leaving her father there for his conference, they continued on to the downtown section where her mother parked the car in front of a little fabric shop.

"I'm going to take the boys over there for some sneakers," she explained, pointing to a shoestore across the street. "Why don't you go in here, Holly, and pick out some material for a summer dress?"

"But I spent all my June allowance on my new bathing suit," Holly reminded her, wishing now she had never made the purchase.

Her mother opened her handbag. "Just a little thanks for all you've been doing."

"Five dollars!" noted Hugh enviously as she handed Holly a bill.

"Lucky duck!" added Roy.

"Now, boys, we buy all your clothes and Holly has to make hers," her mother reminded them. "Besides, you're both getting new sneakers."

[15]

Inside the shop Holly temporarily lost herself in the wonderland of patterns, textures, and colors. There was such an enticing scent about fabrics—one that was a little hard to put into words, but it was sharply clean and, to her, most inspiring. Even handling cloth made her eager to get at the work of designing, draping, and sewing. The choice was difficult, but finally she settled on a brown and green and yellow piqué print that went well with her hair and eyes.

Her mother and brothers weren't in sight when she came out; so she put her package in the car, started slowly down the street on a window-shopping expedition. It was more than silly, she realized now, the state of mind she'd been in about Mark. What was there so special about her that he should have come running after her? Of course she liked to feel that she was special and just a little different—a person who intrigued everyone she met. But did the way she pictured herself inside show outside? In her thoughts she was usually vivacious and gay; but somehow with people she was always a little stiff, a little more serious than she meant to be. If only she could cultivate the lighter touch!

Back at the house there was mail awaiting them. Hugh, who had taken over the role of family postman, brought it in from the rural-free-delivery box by the road—one of the frequent letters from Professor Roberts and, for all of them, an envelope with an imprinted AZALEA ACRES. In it was a warm note from Alice Fairchild.

"Do come to the garden party Saturday, all of you," her mother read aloud, and Holly felt better to think they had been invited. "It's for the benefit of the Quaker Farms church and we're having all kinds of activities," she went on, "swimming, boating, an auction, a white-elephant sale, entertainers, refreshments; and, for the children, pony rides, an old-fashioned hay ride, and games."

Roy's eyes lit up. "Boy, pony rides!"

"Kid stuff," put in Hugh.

"Honestly, Hugh, must you always take a dim view of everything?" Holly remonstrated.

"Look who's talking!"

"What do you mean?"

"You've been an old gloomypuss just because Mark hasn't been up to see you."

"Hugh Elliot, you have the greatest old imagination of anyone I ever saw! Who says I even want to see him?"

"Children! Children!" admonished their mother. "I think it's very nice of the Fairchilds to invite us and I know we'll all have a good time."

"I may have to work," observed their father, who was now reading his letter from Professor Roberts.

"On Saturday afternoon, Walter?" Mrs. Elliot's voice held a hint of disappointment.

"Well," he conceded, "maybe I could go down for a little while."

Holly was of two minds. Should she go or stay home? Of course in a mob scene it wouldn't look as though she were going down to see Mark. But would she really have any fun? Just then the phone in the hall rang.

Hugh rushed to answer, then returned with a leering grin to announce it was for her.

As she suspected, it was Mark.

"Do you realize it's exactly four days since we met?" he wanted to know.

"Is it?" she observed in an it-makes-no-difference-to-me tone, but she couldn't help feeling pleased that he, too, had kept track of the time.

"Honestly," he went on, "I thought I'd be seeing you long before this, but getting ready for the garden party has kept me on the jump."

"I've been very busy myself," she informed him coolly.

"Not too busy to come to the shindig here?" Mark's tone was anxious.

"I'll think about it," she answered.

"I wish I weren't tied up tonight," he apologized, "but after dinner Mr. Fairchild and I have to go down to Quaker Farms and Oxford Center to get a couple of truckloads of benches. And tomorrow night we have to pick up stuff for the auction."

"My next two evenings are taken up too," Holly informed him.

There was a brief silence at the other end of the wire. Then Mark exploded, "All I can say is, tell him that, starting next week, he can expect some competition!"

Holly hung up with her morale vastly improved. She really had Mark worried now. Fortunately he didn't know that her date the next two nights would be with a sewing machine to make a dress for Saturday.

CHAPTER

3

The day of the garden party couldn't have been more perfect. By mid-afternoon, when Holly and her family walked down the hill to Azalea Acres, the slope that rose behind the Fairchilds' guest house across the road from the pink house was already filled with a sea of cars, a surprising sight away off here in the country. From behind the fence and shrubbery came the sound of music and the hum of many voices. Just inside the gate stood Alice Fairchild to greet them, and, beside her, a tall, spare man who topped even her statuesque build.

"This is my husband, Clem," she said, then added, "Darling, these are our new neighbors, the Elliots," and she identified them all in turn.

"I'm very glad to know you," he acknowledged in a voice as warm as his wife's. But, unlike hers, his black eyes had a penetrating look Holly found quite disconcerting.

While her parents chatted with Mr. Fairchild, Holly handed his wife a small, tissue-wrapped package. "We didn't have any white elephants, so I made these for the auction," she explained.

As their hostess untied it, Holly noticed a slight, balding little man standing within earshot watching with absorbed attention.

"Crocheted earrings with sea-shell trim. Wonderful! I'll give them to the auctioneer right away."

But before Mrs. Fairchild could carry out her intention,

the little man had moved in on them. "You know, those would make a good mail-order item."

Alice Fairchild smiled. "Oh, Mr. Ames. This is Holly Elliot. Holly, Mr. Ames is an editor."

"How do you do?" she greeted him. Then, while the mistress of the pink house made her way to a big, bespectacled man who was rearranging lamps and other assorted items on a large table, Holly asked what magazine he edited.

"The *Home Handcrafter*."

"Oh." She didn't want to tell him she'd never heard of it, but he had been encouraged by her question.

"Yes, it's a great little publication," he continued. "Really sort of a clearing house, you might say—information for people who are just starting out in mail order selling the things they make; articles to help those already in business, including success stories—and ads, endless ads offering raw materials and finished handmades and handwork gadgets for sale. You'd be surprised at the number of people in remote spots, as well as in big cities, who earn a full- or part-time living through their mailbox."

While he spoke, Holly took in the details of their surroundings—the string quartet of elderly ladies playing before a backdrop of boxwood, with an artist off to one side sketching them; people sitting on benches, watching, chatting; the kaleidoscopic motion of people going up and coming down the stone steps that led to the terraces on either side of the house. And then, just when she was wondering where Mark might be, he emerged under a cascade of oddly assorted boxes and headed toward the auctioneer. She knew he didn't see her. When or if he did, what would his reaction be after the rather highhanded way she had spoken to him over the phone? Then she realized that Mr. Ames was asking her a question.

"Have you ever tried to sell your earrings?"

"No. I make them for presents."

"No law against trying to sell them too," he chuckled. "You might make a good thing out of it, advertising in one of the mail-order magazines. I'm not saying it would have to be mine," he added with a self-conscious little laugh, "but we certainly wouldn't have any objection to handling your advertising. The classified section is only ten cents a word and there are special rates for yearly insertion."

Holly nodded. This was so boring. She didn't have the slightest interest in mail order. If she hadn't brought the earrings, she might never have been stuck with Mr. Ames. Off in the distance she could see Mr. Fairchild introducing her parents to various small groups. The boys had long since disappeared over the brow of the hill that sloped down from the house. Then, just as she was wondering how she could gracefully get away, Alice Fairchild returned.

"Have you had refreshments yet, Mr. Ames?"

"Very well taken care of, thank you."

"Then if you'll excuse us—" and she guided Holly toward the south terrace. "If I'm not mistaken, our editor friend was trying to sell you on the idea of some space in his magazine."

Holly nodded and managed a humorous smile.

"Now I want to introduce you to someone you'll really enjoy." They had reached the terrace and she led Holly to a long glass table presided over by two hostesses, coffee on one end, punch on the other. Seated before the punch bowl was a petite, vivacious-looking brunette wearing a wreathlike hat made of real flowers and a scoop-necked fuchsia dress.

"Lottie, I'd like you to meet Holly Elliot, who has just moved into the neighborhood. Holly, this is Mrs. Blaine, who runs the Wagon Wheel gift shop over in Woodbury."

"Oh!" Happy astonishment filled her voice. "We passed your shop the other day. I'm dying to see it."

"Holly makes beautiful crocheted earrings. She brought some over for the auction." With that Alice Fairchild left them.

Mrs. Blaine handed her a cup of punch. "So you like to make things too." Holly was surprised at her voice, so full of enthusiasm and bubbling over with inner laughter.

"What do you make?" Holly wanted to know.

"Silver jewelry—only I don't have much time, what with running the shop."

Other people were queuing up behind Holly. "Help yourself to some sandwiches and cakes," Mrs. Blaine invited. "I'll be relieved soon and I'll see you then."

"Yes," smiled Holly, and headed toward the back of the house for a glimpse of the lake and to check up on the boys. Just outside the screened-in rear terrace she almost collided with someone coming out with a big tray of cups and saucers.

"Oh, sorry!" she apologized, and looked up to confront Mark.

"Hey, it's you! You did come!" He sounded unexpectedly pleased. "Wait a minute while I get rid of these and I'll be with you."

But he had no sooner rejoined her than a little girl came

[22]

running up and said Mr. Lorimer wanted him.

"That's the auctioneer," he explained to Holly. "Guess he's about ready to start—darn my luck anyhow. Don't go away, will you?"

For answer Holly gave him an enigmatic smile, but she felt good. Walking down the freshly mowed slope behind the house, she scanned the partly tree-encircled lake which was larger than she had supposed. Though it was some distance below, she thought she recognized Hugh rowing a boatload of smaller children; but soon she saw she was mistaken, for he was installed in a small booth marked CASHIER. Trust him to get in on something like that. Then Roy came into view riding in a pony cart. It looked as though they were both happily occupied.

In the formal garden off to the right, a ballet dancer had just finished entertaining the crowd and was running off to a burst of applause. Now everyone turned expectantly toward the auctioneer, who was hammering for attention with his gavel. Holly took a seat on a rear bench from which she could keep an eye on everything—including her parents, who were in animated conversation with a small group of people, and Mark, who was standing by up front.

Slowly the auction droned on and people began leaving. The only thing that kept Holly interested was her earrings. Almost toward the very last the man directing the auction held up both pairs.

"What am I bid for these?" he asked. "The cards say 'handmade.'"

"Ten cents," offered a fat, gum-chewing little girl in a rocking chair.

"Anyone top that?"

There was silence.

Again the auctioneer turned to the girl. "That the best you can do?"

"It's all I have left."

"Ten cents has it."

Holly watched with a nightmarish sensation as Mark brought them over to the young bidder. After her expectations this was a little hard to take.

"Hi, how are you doing?"

She looked up as Lottie Blaine seated herself on the bench beside her.

"Not so good," she admitted. She really hadn't expected to see her new acquaintance again this afternoon, and this friendly gesture of searching her out put her in a tell-all mood. The next thing she knew she was relating the sad tale of the earrings.

"That's a shame, but things don't always bring what they should at auctions," Mrs. Blaine reassured her. "I've been at enough of them to know. Sometimes things are a steal and other times they're too steep."

"Do you get the things you sell at auctions?"

"Some. Quite a few are on consignment."

"What's 'on consignment'?"

"Craftsmen bring or send me samples of their work and, if I decide it's an item I want to handle, I order a stated amount. But I don't pay them until I've made a sale, and then I get twenty per cent of the proceeds."

"That sounds like a good system."

Lottie Blaine nodded. "Yes, and it's pretty much standard

[24]

practice in gift shops. One way of keeping down the over-head." She consulted her wrist watch, and the many silver bracelets she wore made a musical tinkling. "Oh, dear! I didn't realize it was this late. I've got to get back to the shop. I've kept it locked up long enough."

"Don't you have anyone to help you?" Your husband, she wanted to add; but some impulse kept her quiet.

Mrs. Blaine got up. "No, but I manage pretty well usually. Come see me, won't you?"

"Next week—soon as I can manage a ride over."

"Good! And make it in the evening if that's better for you. I'm generally through in the shop by eight. Just call to make sure I'm around. I go to the summer shows at Westport every week."

"But isn't that far from here?"

"Only a forty-minute drive."

"Is *that* all?"

Her companion laughed. "You sound surprised. Did you think this was way off in the wilds?"

"You live right in the center of Woodbury though."

"Sometimes I think I'm too accessible—but it is a good lo-cation for business. Well, it's been awfully nice meeting you." The way she said it, Holly knew she really meant it.

"It's been wonderful meeting you too."

"See you *soon!*" With a final jaunty wave she headed for the gate.

Holly felt glad she had met Lottie Blaine. That lively young woman radiated a contagious enthusiasm that added a quality of excitement to everything. Looking toward the auctioneer's table, she saw that Mark was busy helping count

[25]

HOUSE OF HOLLY

money. The afternoon seemed to have reached a dead end.
Now, seeing her parents move down the walk to take their
leave, she decided to join them.

"Must you go?" asked Alice Fairchild when her mother
told her what a lovely party it had been.

"Walter has to work."

"That's too bad. I was hoping you could have supper
with us."

"That's very kind of you."

"I enjoyed it too," Holly put in. "And I liked Mrs. Blaine
so much. What does her husband do?"

"She doesn't have a husband. She's a widow."

"Oh." She had been right in heeding that instinct to keep
quiet. If *she* were a widow, she couldn't imagine herself acting so cheerful. Perhaps . . . Then she realized Alice Fairchild was talking to her.

"Can't you stay to supper, Holly?"

"I—" Automatically she looked at her parents, a hangover
from childhood she found hard to break. "It's sweet of you,
but you've had such a big day already."

"Nonsense! It's going to be buffet and you could help me
set it up."

"I'd love to."

Then Mrs. Fairchild asked if the boys might stay also.

"All I can say is, you're a glutton for punishment,'
chuckled her father as he and her mother started up the
road.

By the time noses were counted, there were sixteen for
supper. "I still think the boys and I ought to go home when

I'm through helping," protested Holly as she began carrying plates to the patio.

Alice Fairchild followed with a chest of silverware. "My dear, I'd counted on at least twenty-five," and she indicated the kitchen where Helen, the Polish woman who helped her, was carving a huge ham. Soon Holly was busy fetching and carrying, and she felt as though she and Mrs. Fairchild were friends of long standing.

Sometime later Mark came into the screened-in back terrace while she was carrying a salad bowl to the table.

"What have we here?" he teased. "The new upstairs maid?"

"Mark, behave yourself or you won't get to sit next to Holly," laughingly warned Alice Fairchild.

"You mean she's staying to supper?"

"What do you think? Now you and Clem can start carrying extra chairs out on the south terrace. We're almost ready."

Early the following morning the phone rang. When Holly answered, someone was whistling "Heartbeat"—the current number-one favorite on the hit parade.

"Hi, Holly."

"Good morning, Mark."

"It's a grand day. Would you be in the mood for a beach picnic?"

"I might be persuaded."

"Well, consider yourself persuaded."

"What beach did you have in mind?"

"I can have the station wagon today. Sherwood Island Park over in Westport."

"What do you want me to bring?"

"Only yourself—and your brothers."

"My brothers?" Astonishment filled her voice. Somehow she had been under the impression that this was going to be a twosome.

"Oh, they're cute little rats." Mark seemed unaware of her surprise. "I like them. Can you be ready by ten?" Just like that, thought Holly. Oh, well, the boys will enjoy it at any rate.

The boys were almost beside themselves at the news.

"Wouldn't you like to go too?" Holly asked her parents. It would serve Mark right if they accepted. But her mother shook her head.

"Thanks, dear, but Dad and I will enjoy a nice restful day at home."

"See that the young man takes it easy," observed her father. "I hope he's a good driver."

"Dad, the Fairchilds wouldn't let him take their car if he weren't." Then she hurried to pack the new bathing suit and some towels.

On the way to the beach Holly hugged her side of the front seat.

Mark looked over at her. "I don't bite," he grinned.

"It's a warm day."

"If you ask me, it's rather chilly."

"Think so?"

But soon she was caught up in the delight of the lovely day, the pleasure of getting away and driving through unfamiliar surroundings.

After what seemed like miles, with Holly eagerly scanning the landscape for signs of artists with easels—perversely there weren't any—the road began paralleling an inlet filled with small boats. Soon they were crossing it on a bridge and Mark announced that this was Sherwood Island. Far down, ahead of them, they could see rows of parked cars and woods filled with picnic tables. Then the breeze came their way and they began to smell the sharp, tantalizing salt air and glimpse blue slashes of water between the trees.

"What'll it be first, gang, eating or swimming?" Mark wanted to know as he parked.

"Let's eat!" chorused the boys and, while they changed into swim shorts in one of the little bathhouses, Holly helped Mark set out the picnic lunch Alice Fairchild had put up.

After the meal Mark announced he was taking the boys surf-casting farther down the beach. Just as though I were an elderly chaperon or a fifth wheel, thought Holly, changing into her white sharkskin suit. He hadn't even asked if she'd like to come along. Not that she would have. What she was in the mood for was sun bathing so she'd get a good start on her summer tan, then a salt-water dip. She had at least imagined Mark would contrive for some time alone with her. Placing her beach towel on the sand, Holly patted some sun lotion on her face and arms, put on her sunglasses, lay down, and closed her eyes. One thing was sure. This was the first and last time she would go anywhere with Mark Logan.

"Hi, Sleeping Beautiful."

Holly opened a surprised eye to see Mark grinning down at her.

[29]

"Well, looks like I got the kids out of our hair for a while." He sat down on the sand facing her. "Do you realize we haven't even had a good chance for a talk since we met?"

Now she was sorry she'd been so quick to criticize him. "What do you want to talk about?"

"You."

"What's there to talk about me?"

"Well, for one thing, what a restful person you are—not feeling you have to keep up a stream of chatter every minute like some girls."

Strange to be flattered when her silences grew out of stiffness and shyness, and sometimes, like today, even pique.

"Of course there's something else rather disturbing about you, Holly."

"Oh?"

"A fellow doesn't quite know where he's at with you— what you're thinking."

"You haven't known me very long," she reminded him, managing an impish smile.

"Give me time."

"I don't know very much about you either. What are you majoring in at college?"

"Meteorology. I'm studying to go into the weather bureau."

"Not too many people go into that, do they?"

"No. And still fewer where I want to work."

"Where's that?"

"Alaska."

His intention was such a surprise that Holly sat up. "Alaska!" She looked across the shimmering water, marked

[30]

the slow passage of a haze-dimmed sailboat on the horizon. "That's a long way off."

"Not so far by plane."

"But why Alaska?"

He chuckled. "I went there for a vacation with my folks the summer I was twelve, and didn't want to come back. Since then I've read pretty much everything that's been written about it."

Holly put on her bathing cap, dimming the deep-throated, rhythmical whoosh of the surf as it pounded ashore. "Do you have any brothers or sisters?"

"No, worse luck. That way all the attention gets focused on me."

They were interrupted by excited shouts, and now Hugh and Roy came racing up with a good-sized fish flopping about in a pail. Their time alone was at an end.

Later, on the way home, Holly felt pleasantly relaxed. It had been a better day than she had anticipated, and Mark had managed time alone with her. She suspected that, if her brothers hadn't interrupted when they did, the conversation might have become even more interesting. How he really felt about her though was a great big question mark. Alone in her room later that night, she again reviewed their day together. Someone restful to talk to, to swim with—was that all there was to it? That part about her being disturbing—had he really meant it? But when it came to Mark's clear-cut career plans which included Alaska, she envied him. Maddeningly enough, she herself had no idea what store she would be working in this fall and, until the family moved to Watertown, she couldn't even start her job hunting.

CHAPTER

4

Even through the window the Wagon Wheel gift shop looked inviting. When Holly opened the screen door to go in, a bell jingled somewhere in the interior of the house and Lottie Blaine's cheery "Be right with you!" welcomed her. A moment later she came down a stairway that led right into the shop, and her exuberance filled the room.

"Holly Elliot! How nice to see you! I've had you on my mind ever since the garden party."

"I wanted to come sooner," Holly apologized, "but this is really the first chance I've had to stop." The family always seemed to be in a hurry when they went by here on the way to marketing or house hunting over in Watertown. Then last week when Mark had her out for a drive and she suggested going in, he had vetoed the idea. Gift shops, it seemed, were among his pet hates because his mother haunted them and cluttered up the house with what he termed horrible doodads and antique junk.

"Someone drop you off?" Lottie Blaine asked.

"Yes. Mrs. Fairchild. She had some errands in Woodbury."

"Could you stay for lunch?"

Holly thanked her but said that Alice Fairchild would be back for her in a short while and that her family had plans for the afternoon.

"Another time then. But come in and sit down." Leading the way to a cozy, book-lined room with a fireplace half screened by a wallpaper fan, she indicated a comfortable chair. "What have you been doing that's fun?"

Her very attitude seemed to color the summer with excitement and Holly found herself describing in glowing terms some of the things she had been doing with Mark with and without benefit of her brothers, who were still included in some of their activities. In fact, looking back on some of the times, she found herself retelling them with humor, and Lottie Blaine laughed appreciatively.

"I would have loved having younger brothers too," she was saying just as the shop bell jingled again. "I'll be back soon," she smiled, getting to her feet.

"I'd like to see the shop too," put in Holly. "I thought I might pick out some things for Christmas."

"For goodness sakes, don't think you have to buy!"

"I know that, but I want to."

There were so many things that caught Holly's eye she didn't know where to look first—woodenware, decorated and plain; ceramics of all kinds; jewelry; hand-painted napkins and matched luncheon sets; unusual lamps and crackled glassware; conversation-making gadgets, such as a tiny flit gun designed for a purse atomizer. This latter she couldn't resist even though her allowance wasn't geared to frivolities. She'd use it on Mark the next time they went out—which would be tonight.

"One thing I can't understand," she remarked as Lottie Blaine was wrapping up her purchases, "is how you know what sort of things to stock."

Her acquaintance smiled. "Well, there are certain gift-shop categories people look for—personal and decorative accessories that are nice for yourself, your own home, and for gifts. And if you can have some exclusives—items especially made for you, the entire output of a certain craftsman—you have a good drawing card. Also it gives you something special to feature if you have a mail-order business."

"Do you?" Holly asked in surprise.

"Yes. I run an ad every month in *Hobbies* magazine. Of course," she added, "with me it's just a side line, but you'd be surprised at the number who just specialize in mail order."

Holly listened politely, but her mind was on a trip to New Haven her father had promised them that afternoon. A moment later Alice Fairchild came in to say she was ready.

"I'm sure Clem will try to get home this afternoon in time for a dip," she observed on the way home.

"Doesn't he like New York?"

"Not in summer."

Mr. Fairchild had his own accounting business and kept books for various firms in Connecticut and metropolitan New York. In winter his assignments also included a number of citrus groves in Florida and some sugar plantations in Cuba, so he and his wife combined those trips with their vacation—pretty much of a dream setup, Holly had decided.

As they passed Azalea Acres, Mark, who was clipping a privet hedge across the street by the guest house, grinned and waved at them.

"We feel very fortunate to have Mark help us out in summer," commented Mrs. Fairchild as they continued up the hill. "It's unusual to find a boy in his position working at all—and he's been taking jobs ever since he was thirteen. His father has a factory, a big brass foundry, and has done extremely well. Or has Mark told you?"

"No." From the bits he had thrown out, she had assumed his father was a skilled worker in a factory.

"That's typical of him. He's reticent about a lot of things."

Does he talk about me? Holly wanted to ask, but didn't. The more she saw of Mark, the more she liked him; but there was evident tension between him and his folks. She might have problems, but strained family relations was not one of them.

Back home she discovered a state of uproar. Right after she had left that morning, a beautiful misty gray Maltese kitten had appeared on the scene and made itself very much at home. The boys were so excited that they didn't even want to go to New Haven.

"He might get lonesome and run away if we went," explained Roy.

"Besides, we've got to build him a house," added Hugh.

"The kitten might belong to someone in the neighborhood," their mother cautioned.

"We haven't seen any cat like this around." This protest from Roy.

"I guess maybe someone dropped him out of a car," offered Hugh.

Their father looked from the kitten to the boys and back

[35]

to the kitten. "Well, just so there's no fuss if anyone comes to claim him—or if he runs away."

The boys promised and clung to their decision to stay home. For Holly, after weeks in the country, the trip to New Haven was a special treat. While her father went to do research at the Yale University library, she and her mother separated to do some errands.

Presently, armed with Alaskan travel folders and unusual dime-store buttons she would make into earrings, Holly went to the biggest local department store, where she was to meet her mother. Inside the revolving doors she paused to look around. This was her kind of atmosphere—the purposeful hustle and bustle of shoppers; the charming, well-groomed salesgirls behind the counters with their attractive display of fashion merchandise; the bong-bong of the chimelike store bells that sounded at frequent intervals; the enticing whiff of sprayed perfume that hovered around the toiletries counter; the whimsical starfish and other handmade seaside props that swung overhead, adding to the illusion of coolness. She loved a store in summertime, wintertime, anytime, and in this joyous mood she took an elevator upstairs to help her mother select some of the dresses she'd need for faculty affairs at Taft.

On the return trip her father made things interesting by taking them over a new route—the Derby Turnpike, which soon paralleled water.

"What river is this?" her mother wanted to know as they crossed it on a bridge leading into the town of Derby.

"The Housatonic. From here on, it flows down to Bridgeport and out to Long Island Sound."

At Stevenson Dam they took the by-now-familiar woodland road that would eventually connect with Goodhill Road, where they lived. By and by her father sighed.

"Tired after your library session, dear?" her mother wanted to know.

"It's not that. I was thinking about the house situation. We'll have to decide on a place soon, so we can move in by the first of September."

"If only rents weren't so expensive!" worried her mother.

"Oh, we'll find something," Holly airily assured them, even though up to now they had always lived in quarters provided by the various schools where her parents had taught.

As they drove into the yard, the boys came running to meet them. "Wait till you see our cat apartment house!" they cried.

"Upstairs for sleeping, downstairs for eating," amended Roy.

The three of them admired the upended orange crate in which the kitten lay in a contented curve, paw under chin.

"The mail come?" her father inquired now.

"Yes, it's in the living room. Want me to get it, Dad?" offered Hugh.

"Thanks, but I'm going in to put on something cooler." Minutes later, still in street clothes, he reappeared waving a letter. "I think this may be the answer to our house problem."

"Who's it from, Walter?"

"Professor Roberts, Louise. Here's your mail, Holly—one of your craft magazines."

"Oh, thanks, Dad."

"Darling, don't keep us in suspense."

"Well, it seems Roberts has received a renewal of his fellowship—this time to work in South America—and he won't be back home for another year. Meanwhile he'd like to rent the house to reliable people and we could have it very reasonably."

"Isn't it rather far for you to commute?"

"Only about forty minutes. That isn't bad."

"Well . . ." Her mother's face began to brighten.

Aghast, Holly looked from one to the other. "Mother—Dad—you wouldn't seriously consider staying here!"

"Why not? What's wrong with it?" her father wanted to know.

"It's nicer than a lot of places we could get in town," her mother pointed out.

"But it's so far away from everything! And how could I get back and forth to a job in the city?"

"We can work out all those details later," her parents assured her, but Holly was not to be consoled. The day, which had been so happy and bright up to now, was ruined. The helpless, marooned feeling she had had at the start of the summer began to overwhelm her again. Next month, with Mark gone, this place would be as bad as a desert island. To hide the gathering tears of frustration, she ran into the house.

Just as she started up the stairs, the phone rang. It was Mark to say that Mr. Fairchild had returned early and they could have the station wagon any time. How would she like to go out to dinner, to some place special, perhaps to the French Bite on the way to Woodbury? Holly didn't feel very celebrationy, but at least it would be better than sitting out a meal with the family.

. On the drive over to the main road, Mark noticed her downcast mood.

"Problems?" he inquired.

"That's one way of saying it!" And then she told him about her parents' decision to stay in Oxford.

"Is that bad?"

"It certainly isn't good as far as my career goes!"

Mark looked at her out of laughing eyes. "Sugar, a girl like you doesn't have to worry about a career."

"Why not?" she challenged.

"It's all cut out for you—marriage."

"A girl needs something in addition to marriage!"

"You sound as though that were something you learned out of a copybook."

"Well, it isn't!" she defended, even though she had been brought up on the precept. "Just look at all the women who are at loose ends after their children grow up, if they don't have a special interest."

Then he asked a most unexpected question. "Holly, how would you like to live in Alaska?"

CHAPTER

5

Holly was too surprised for words. After treating her in what had amounted to big-brotherly fashion all summer, Mark was now going romantic on her. All in the same instant she had been flattered and frightened. Life had been so safe and sheltered even if it had had its dull moments, and now adventuresome vistas in a far-off place were opening out. She, it seemed, was the girl with whom Mark most wanted to share his life in Alaska once he was out of college and working for the weather bureau.

"Holly, let's get engaged," he begged.

"Mark, we're too young to be going steady."

"Don't act so darn sensible! Lots of people our age are married—even have children."

"I know. But you're studying for a career," she reminded him. "And then there's mine to think about," she added silently.

"Don't you love me?" he challenged.

"I—" Her mind was in a whirl. This was all so sudden, so unexpected. To be engaged. What would her parents say? And yet did it matter what they thought? They weren't taking her wishes into account staying here in Oxford! A secret engagement was a temptation.

"Mark, I didn't even know how you felt about me," she told him, sparring for time, trying to hold onto this wonderful moment, and wanting at the same time to be honest. "Maybe you'll meet someone you like even better," she added.

"Are you trying to tell me there's someone else?"

She was on the verge of saying "No;" then she looked up at him, her eyes twin pinpoints of mischief.

"Just wait. You'll see I'm the guy for you."

In the remaining weeks of summer he was doubly attentive. In fact, they had such a wonderful time together that it was rather a shock to Holly when she realized it was time for him to go back to college. Having Mark around had become an accepted part of her existence here on Goodhill Road.

But on this afternoon in late September, just thinking about their last date together made her smile reminiscently. The house was filled with people, but Mark up at M.I.T. had more reality for her than they. With Alice Fairchild as cohostess, her mother was holding open house to meet the women who lived in the surrounding countryside.

One of the last to arrive was Lottie Blaine. "Never thought I'd get away from the shop," she apologized. "Every time I start to lock up, someone arrives!"

"What you need, dear, is an assistant," Alice Fairchild pointed out.

"I'd love one, but assistants come high—too much so for me, I'm afraid." And then to Holly, "Brought you this—it's one of the magazines I sometimes advertise in—run by two awfully nice gals in Michigan. Thought you might find some new sources of supply for some of your craft projects."

Holly thanked her, noting that it was a multigraphed publication, with a picture cover, entitled *Hodgepodge*; then she put it aside for later, to help with the serving. This had been a week of parties. Yesterday had been Hugh's birthday and a dozen of his and Roy's friends had been over for a picnic supper. Since he liked crafts as much as Holly, she had given him something he had wanted for a long time— a spatter gun for spatter stenciling, with an assortment of screw-on paints and stencil paper. All morning and for quite a while after lunch he had been locked up in his room working with the set. She couldn't imagine why he should want to be so secretive, but that was his privilege.

A short while later, as she was circulating with a round wooden tray of dainty sandwiches, the boys came in, each with a sheaf of handbills they began passing out. Holly noted smiles, then straight faces as the papers were tucked into handbags.

"Got one for me, Roy?" she asked on her way to the kitchen.

"Nope—all used up," he stated, quickly following Hugh out.

"Mother, what was on those sheets the boys handed out?" she wanted to know her next time around.

"I didn't see one, dear."

"Oh." Well, whatever it was, it must have been funny. Also, she wondered, why had everybody put it away so promptly? Knowing the boys and their tricks, she couldn't help being suspicious.

A few minutes later, arranging tiny cupcakes on a platter at the kitchen table, she looked up to see Hugh standing outside the screened window with Misty, the kitten, in his arms.

"Hugh, what was on those papers you boys passed out?" she demanded.

"Wouldn't you like to know?" he teased, then vanished.

A suspicion grew that the handbills had something to do with her. There might be another way to find out. As soon as she had passed the cupcakes and more sandwiches, Holly hurried upstairs to her brothers' room. The door was unlocked. There on the floor beside the upended spatter gun lay a much-spattered sheet of stencil paper into which Hugh had cut three words in bold capital letters.

HOLLY
LOVES
MARK

How dared he do anything like this! And for him to choose a time when all these women were here—many whom she and her mother had just met for the first time. Almost more embarrassing though was having Alice Fairchild and Lottie Blaine see it. After this, how could she possibly go downstairs again?

From below came her mother's voice, summoning her.

Trying hard not to look self-conscious, Holly rejoined the women. After a while she managed to catch Lottie Blaine alone.

"Did you see the little gem my brothers turned out?"

"I didn't know if you knew. I still think I missed out on a lot of fun not having younger brothers," she smiled.

"Well, I wish to goodness my brothers would grow up! The things I have to put up with from them!"

"It's all part of the fun."

But Holly didn't share her view. Waiting until the family was seated at dinner, she sprang her trap.

"Do you know the thanks I got for giving Huge a stencil set?" she demanded of her parents. And then she related what he and Roy had done.

"Boys, you didn't!" There was reproof in her mother's voice.

"She's just an old tattletale!" exploded Roy.

Hugh held his ground. "I only put down what's so."

"Hugh Elliot, whatever gave you the idea that I—"

But her brother was ready with an interruption. "Do Mother and Dad know that you have Mark's identification bracelet in your jewel case?"

"You little beast! You've been snooping in *my* private property!"

"I notice *your* bracelet's gone too," he added smugly.

Speechless, Holly turned to face her parents. She was furious at Hugh and now, because of him, there would be a scene. She hadn't meant them to find out quite this way that she and Mark were serious about each other and that they had exchanged bracelets the night before he left. Now she was in for it.

Her father's voice when he spoke was mild. "I'd consider it very odd," he smiled, "if boys didn't want to exchange identification bracelets with Holly."

This ended the argument, even though it was an unexpected turn. But didn't her father and her mother, who also seemed to take it casually, understand that Mark wasn't boys in general but a particular boy? Since his departure he had taken up a large share of her waking thoughts. By now she was even quite used to the idea of Alaska. What she still had to figure out was what she could do up there for a parttime paying interest within four walls of her own. She had no more solution to that than she did to the job situation here at home. It was a question that had even her family stumped, despite their assurances that everything would work out.

Her father's hours were such that he left for the school too late for her to connect with any Waterbury bus, and he came home before the stores closed. No one in the neighborhood went over that way either. A car of her own would be out of the question financially; and when it came to boarding in the city, her family didn't see much sense to that.

"You wouldn't have much cash in hand at the end of the week," her father had pointed out.

"Experience though," she had reminded him.

Her mother had kept out of the discussion. With the boys in school and no classes of her own to teach this year, Holly knew she was glad for company. But Holly kept telling herself, I can't mark time forever!

After the dishes were done she went up to her room with the mail and the magazine Lottie Blaine had given her. Seated on the studio couch that was her bed, she opened a large envelope marked *Home Handcrafter*. Mr. Ames, persistent little man, had sent her a complimentary copy—also an ad contract to be filled out. She threw it down and had begun leafing through *Hodgepodge* with its readable little columns, how-to information articles, and countless ads when she was interrupted by a sharp rap on the door.

"Come in!" she called.

The door was pushed slightly ajar, then a shallow, squarish box was shoved into the room.

"Take your old thing! I don't want it!" proclaimed Hugh.

Even as she heard him pelting down the stairs, she recognized the stencil set; but for the moment it could stay there, since an item had just caught her eye.

> Handmade Alaskan rag dolls. Indian, Eskimo, prospector, and dance-hall belle, $2 each. Satisfaction guaranteed. Send orders to Tansy Adams, Box 28, Sitka, Alaska.

Here was a girl or woman—in Alaska of all places—who was establishing a contact with an outside market by way of mail order. Was this the answer for her too?

CHAPTER

6

"Miss!" The voice crackled out in sharp authority. "What do you think you're doing?"

Holly, picking sprays of red berries from a bush by the roadside leading down to Jackson's Cove, looked up to see an unsmiling young man get out of a car and come over to her.

"Don't you realize that black alder—Connecticut holly—is scarce and on the conservation list?" he demanded.

She managed an indignant "No!" Then, seeming to read what was on her mind, he added, "I'm one of the state conservation officers."

Even if he was, did he have to be so smug about it? She wished Mark had been here. He would have told him off in no uncertain terms. But all she could do was to say in what she hoped was a sarcastic tone, "You don't mind if I take the ones I've already picked?"

His mouth was still set in a straight line. "You might as well. They're past saving!"

He had come up as suddenly as a thundercloud—and he looked like one, too, with his dark hair, dark eyes, and heavy dark shell-rimmed glasses. If she never saw him again, it would be too soon. Now he was addressing her again.

"You realize of course, don't you, that if I pressed charges you would be liable to a twenty-five-dollar fine?"

"No," she stammered, then, without a further look in his direction, started for the corner and home. Twenty-five dollars! What a calamity that would be! Here she was trying so hard to make some money and in the process she had almost been penalized. At the corner where his car passed her, heading downhill, she didn't even glance his way.

It would be November before her first mail-order ad for her earrings would appear in *Hodgepodge*, because copy had to be in a whole month ahead of time. And the one she was running in *Home Handcrafter*, which had a six-week deadline, wouldn't even come out until December. Meanwhile, knowing it would be some time before she got any income from those ads, she wanted to earn something, so she had made up fifty pairs of assorted earrings and had left them on consignment at the Wagon Wheel. When she mentioned unusual dried bouquets and corsages as another item, Lottie Blaine had said it sounded like a good idea—and that's what she had been working on today until the unwelcome interruption.

Passing Azalea Acres, she looked for a glimpse of Alice Fairchild so she could tell her what had happened. But the garage was empty and the station wagon gone. Arriving home, she found a note on the kitchen table asking her to put the casserole dish in the oven at four-thirty and she remembered that this was her mother's afternoon to play den mother to the Cub Scouts of which Roy was a member. Upstairs in her room she brought out Mark's latest letter to reread it.

Hi, Sugar. At this point the old grind has become routine again. I'd much rather be back in Connecticut with you. Two whole years till I get the old sheepskin. Sometimes I wonder if I'll hold out that long. There's a new book out on Alaska I thought you'd like to read. Bought it at a bookstore in Boston for you the other day and they're sending it on.

She was looking forward to it, but right now she was still seething at the state conservationist. With no one to talk to, she picked up her pen.

"It isn't that I object to conservation," she wrote Mark, "and I certainly wouldn't have picked the black alder if I had known it was scarce. But honestly, the way that character from the state acted, you'd think I was a criminal—threatening me with a twenty-five-dollar fine and all!"

After she had it down on paper, she felt better. Then, looking at her clock, she saw it was past time for her to light the oven.

That evening right after dinner it began to rain. It was the cozy kind of family evening Holly loved. Her father had history-test papers to correct; her mother wanted to get caught up on the mending; the boys had some research to do for school. She herself wanted to have an advance stock of earrings ready for her ads, and so she set up a bridge table in the living room. As she laid out her supplies, she couldn't help thinking how surprised Mark would be when he discovered she had a going mail-order business. Imagine opening countless letters, each with an order for a dollar or more!

Of course she had quite an outlay in materials, but some she had inherited.

Her great-great-grandmother and great-great-grandfather Vanderstocken, on her mother's side, had had a Ladies' Notions shop in New York and some of the items remaining when they closed it were cards of buttons, many of them collector's items, which had been handed down in the family. When she first began making button earrings for gifts, her mother had given her a selection and she was going to include some of these antiques among her articles for sale.

Only this week she had received a gross of ear screws in three assorted sizes and in both gilt and nickel finish, ordered from a supplier advertising in *Hodgepodge*. Unscrewing a tube of colorless household cement, she placed a matched pair of leaf-shaped mother-of-pearl buttons under side up and put a blob of the adhesive in the center of each. This done, she selected a medium-sized gilt ear screw and placed it in position, pressing down with her finger. Then she attached an ear screw to the other button in the same way. In an hour they could be handled, in twenty-four hours safely worn without fear of their coming apart. As she was wondering what to make up next, her glance took in her selection of modern buttons, some with embedded rhinestones, others set with simulated jewelstones. Just then the phone rang.

"Holly, dear, will you answer?" asked her mother, and she hurried to take the call. For the space of a heartbeat she thought it might be Mark, but the voice on the other end was Alice Fairchild's.

"Holly, I have the Farm Bureau Christmas Box overnight

and I thought you might like to see it for some ideas."

"What's the Christmas box?" she wanted to know.

Her friend explained that women in the local farm bureaus made up actual samples of gifts complete with patterns and directions and these in turn were sent in to the county bureaus, which made up boxes and circulated them among all the local groups as inspiration for Christmas gift making. "Could you come down?" she added.

"I'd love to."

"Good! Then Rusty and I"—Rusty was their cocker spaniel —"will start up the road to meet you."

The boys would have liked to go along; but their parents vetoed that, saying it would be too late for them.

For Holly the box was a wonderland—a packaged bazaar with directions. Among the many items were a party apron of red tulle with a Christmas-tree motif outlined in tinsel and decorated with sequins, a chubby rag doll dressed like Red Riding Hood, a more slender rag doll with long arms and legs and a tiny waist—Cinderella with a change of wardrobe, which included a house dress and ball gown, textile painted bridge sets, and a Christmas tablecloth with matching napkins that had an unusual touch—clusters of small bells tied to the corners with yarn bows. Alice Fairchild even helped her copy the directions and trace the patterns. She was as interested in helping her with ideas for the mail-order project as though it were her own.

The following day the book from Mark arrived and, while the slow weeks before the first of November ticked off, she concentrated on her study of Alaska. All she read added up to adventure—something she certainly wasn't getting here, where the days marched by in calm procession. But at least there would be a step-up in the tempo of her life once the orders for her ads came pouring in. The only real excitement was when the mailbox held a letter from Mark, when he phoned, or when she dreamed of their future.

Around the first of November, Holly had drawn a big red circle on the calendar. Against that day she held in readiness wrapping paper, string, books of gummed address labels, and even cotton-padded earring boxes she had bought from a supplier. But on the long-looked-for date nothing happened. For over a week she lived in a state of suspended expectancy. Each time she opened the mailbox she looked for a letter or letters addressed to *The Handcrafter, R.F.D. #2, Southbury, Connecticut,* but there just weren't any.

Early one morning in mid-November there was a knock on the door. Alice Fairchild had driven to the post office for her own mail and, thinking they might like theirs too, had brought the Elliots' along. Holly thumbed through it looking for a letter from Mark. It was only after she had put it down that her brain telegraphed her the delayed reaction that there was an envelope addressed to the *Handcrafter.*

The postmark said California and it had been sent air mail. With trembling fingers she tore it open. Enclosed was a crisp, crackling new dollar bill for a pair of her gold metallic crocheted earrings. The log jam had broken and she was in business at last.

The next day there were two letters. Holly could scarcely contain her excitement. But when she opened them, they were from other advertisers who wanted her business. Next to come was an important-looking letter from a great Chicago newspaper.

"Imagine! They're asking me to advertise on their weekly gift page. Anyone would think I was a going concern," she told her mother with a wry little laugh.

"How much does an ad cost?"

"Six dollars and forty cents for the smallest insertion. What they don't realize is that's a lot of money to me. The insertion in *Hodgepodge* and the one still to come out in *Home Handcrafter* had been much less. But now she was beginning to have misgivings about having chosen the right item to advertise. One order! And Lottie Blaine had sold only three pairs of earrings the last time she had heard from her.

Each succeeding day the mail became heavier, but it wasn't the kind she had hoped for. Judging by the contents of the letters and the cards, there were many more people than she had ever dreamed of who offered all kinds of products and handmades and services by mail. Now that her name was out in the public domain by way of her little ad, they were all soliciting her. To say the least, it was rather ironic! Even her romance had to be carried on via the R.F.D. and that was hardly a satisfactory state of affairs. Mark wrote quite often, but on paper he was a person of few words. It was much too long since she had seen him. If only they could be together for a few hours, she knew she would feel better. The trouble was, he had a part-time job—and that left him no time to come down for a visit.

"We'll make up for it during the Christmas vacation," he promised her. But December might as well have been a million years away. If she had been busy, she might not have been so aware of the slow, monotonous passage of the days. As things stood, without orders and without the prospect of any more, she didn't even have an incentive to make up more earrings.

When, several days before Thanksgiving, her father suggested it would be a change for them to eat out on the holiday and then, barring bad weather, take a drive to see more of western Connecticut, Holly welcomed the idea. The Fairchilds were in Cuba and the neighborhood seemed deserted without them.

The way things turned out, the day was clear and very mild for November. They had a leisurely meal at a lovely old inn in the foothills of the Berkshires, then drove until almost dark. Returning home, they found a note clipped under the door knocker. It was for Holly.

Drove down to surprise you with one of the fellows in my class who had to go to Newtown. Waited as long as I could. Sorry to have missed you.

MARK

Missing Mark's visit was the final event in the chain of frustrating circumstances that had made up the fall. Holly was determined it would be the last. From now on she wasn't going to let things happen to her. She was going to make them happen. It was all very well for a magazine like *Hodgepodge* to say it took time to build up a mail-order business. She didn't have very much time—only the two years before Mark finished college—to make her mailbox business a going concern. There must be some good reason for the almost complete lack of response to her ad, and she was determined to find that reason.

With this in mind, the Monday after Thanksgiving she drove in as far as Woodbury with her father to lunch with Lottie Blaine. When she arrived Lottie was opening her mail.

Holly indicated the letters. "Are those all mail order?" she asked.

"Almost all," Lottie told her.

"Do you get that much response every day?"

"Sometimes more—sometimes less. The pre-Christmas season is particularly good."

Holly took a deep breath. "I had only one order from my ad in *Hodgepodge*. I don't think I'll advertise in that any more."

Taking a booklet of address labels from one of the pigeon-holes in her desk, Mrs. Blaine tore one out and inserted it in her typewriter. Then she looked at Holly. "I didn't see an ad by you in the magazine. Was it this month's?"

Holly nodded. "Yes."

"Display ad?"

"What do you mean by that."

"Any ad an inch or more in size that shows up what you have to advertise either by an arrangement of type or by type and artwork."

"Mine was just three lines close together."

"Oh, classified. They're harder to find, though people do dig them out. And one insertion is scarcely a fair test of a magazine's pulling power. It's steady advertising month after month that pays off. Mind if I work as we talk?"

"Of course not."

She started typing out an address. "Once people begin coming into the shop, I have a hard time getting back to my desk work. And I do like to get my mail inquiries answered, and my mail orders packed and off, the same day they come in. You really owe that to your mail-order customers."

"What do people send inquiries about?" Holly wanted to know.

Lottie explained that, in addition to the featured items with prices in her ads, she also offered a free descriptive price list of other things for sale. "Even when I send an order, I always include a price list or small catalogue. What you work for is repeat customers. If people are satisfied with what you send them, and you offer them a choice of other things, chances are they'll order one or more of them."

"But how do I know whether the earrings are the right thing to advertise?"

Just at this point they were interrupted by someone coming in to look around the shop, and Lottie had to leave her. But during their luncheon Holly came back to the question again.

Lottie's face relaxed in a humorous expression. "There's nothing strictly foolproof about mail order—no hard and set rules about 'this will go and that won't.' You have to be prepared for a certain amount of trial and error—try out different leaders."

Holly took another forkful of the delicious baked loaf with lobster sauce. "Do you mean by 'leaders' the things to feature in the ad?"

"Yes. Actually a leader is just a come-on—something to

interest the ad reader in sending for your list of offerings. And even if people don't buy your leader or order from your first list, you have their name and address to add to your mail prospects. Often they'll buy from future mailings."

"I wish I knew all you do about mail order."

Lottie Blaine gave a good-natured laugh. "Just wait till you've had five years' experience!"

Five years! By that time she'd be an established Alaskan resident living goodness knows where with Mark, perhaps in some lonely outpost; and every time the mail came, there would be a great deal for her. Her outgoing mails, too, would be heavy. Meanwhile she still had a business to establish. Without telling Lottie the reason for her urgency, she asked if there wasn't something she could do to speed up the getting-started process.

"Run display ads in as many magazines as you can," Lottie suggested just as the shop bell jingled announcing another visitor.

"But doesn't that cost a lot of money?" Holly asked, reverting to the subject when Lottie returned to serve the dessert.

Lottie smiled. "An inch in one of the big magazines like *American Home* runs into hundreds of dollars, and of course you get a wonderful response; but in lots of the smaller magazines five or ten dollars and up will buy you an inch."

Holly suppressed a sigh. What Lottie didn't realize was that, with her present limited finances, even that amount was out of reach.

Again the doorbell jingled and with an apologetic " 'Scuse, please," Lottie Blaine went out to the shop.

While she was gone Holly cleared the table and washed the dishes. A little later she helped Lottie finish packing hurricane lamps and old-fashioned trivets that had been among the day's orders; then, since her father wasn't calling for her until after four, she offered to take the packages to the post office.

"Would you, Holly? You're an angel!" Lottie exclaimed. "The way people keep coming today, I know I'll never get to the post office myself before closing time."

When she returned, the shop was filled and one woman was even examining her earrings. Holly could see that Lottie was having all she could do to wrap the things her customers had selected.

"Can't I wrap?" she offered, and again Lottie gratefully accepted. Then the phone rang and Holly answered it.

"Lot?" A pleasant masculine voice inquired.

"Just a minute and I'll call Mrs. Blaine."

"Who's this?" the voice wanted to know.

"Holly Elliot, a friend of hers."

"Oh. I thought maybe she had an assistant."

Much more quickly than she had imagined, it was after four and her father was stopping for her. She had enjoyed the day in the shop very much; too, Lottie Blaine had been very generous with her advice. The only trouble was, how to follow it when she didn't even have a shoestring capital. And, if she couldn't make some money through her mailbox, what else could she do, marooned way off in the country miles from the through-traffic routes.

Then, recalling what the man on the phone had said, she had an inspiration. She waited to call Lottie until she was sure the shop would be closed, but she caught her in the middle of her meal.

"I thought I'd never be able to lock up," Lottie remarked in her usual good-humored voice, which still could not hide the drag of fatigue. "Starting the day after Thanksgiving, a lot of people feel Christmas is just around the corner and the rush is on."

"That's just what I had a brain storm about," Holly told her. "You need some help and I need some money. Don't you think we could work something out?"

CHAPTER

7

The Woman's Club was sponsoring an art show. Lottie Blaine was chairman and she asked Holly to act as her stand-in and greet the different artists and sculptors as they came to deliver their work, while she took care of some other details.

Oils and water colors, awaiting hanging, leaned against the length of one wall. The door opened and an artist came in carrying two big frames. Holly introduced herself and showed him where he could leave his pictures.

She watched as he put his water colors against the wall. One was called "End of the Parade" and showed a group of urchins running after the calliope that brought up the circus procession winding into the circus crowds. Just seeing it awakened a nostalgia for her own childhood days when the circus came to town. The other picture was labeled "Dancing at the Beach."

"Isn't that Hampton Beach, New Hampshire?" she asked him, and he seemed pleased by her recognition. Then a famous maker of mobiles whom she had met earlier joined them and, while Holly was doing the honors, Lottie hurried in.

Both men greeted her warmly. Holly marveled at the

range of Lottie's acquaintance, for she had invited a select group of artists and sculptors from out-of-the-way towns as well as from cities all over Connecticut. She had also known just whom to contact for newspaper, radio, and television publicity. Holly envied Lottie her friend-making facility. But, at least, through her she was in on the behind-the-scenes picture of what went into the making of an art exhibit.

Now, not wanting to break into the conversation, she pantomimed that she was going back to the shop. The time had passed so quickly since she had started working at the Wagon Wheel that it was hard to realize this was already the end of her second week and also two weeks nearer Christmas holidays, when Mark would be down and staying at the Fairchilds'.

It was only a short walk to Lottie's house. As she waited for cars to pass so she could cross the street, Holly couldn't help thinking again how lucky she was to have made a job connection that dovetailed with her father's schedule. Also it was a good feeling to know that Lottie Blaine would have called her the same evening, had Holly not phoned first about helping out in the gift shop. For the moment things were going so well that she was holding her breath. With part of the proceeds from her first week's salary she had been able to order display ads—one in *Hodgepodge,* another in *Profitable Hobbies,* each one featuring a different style of fabric handbag. One would appear in January, the other in February. At least this was a start in the right direction.

Unlocking the door of the gift shop, she recalled how naïve she had been the first few days at work. Her prize boner had been to rearrange the stock, putting the all-of-a-kinds together in one location as in a department store. The other had been following visitors around, practically breathing down their necks in her eagerness to write up a sale. When Lottie discovered what she was doing, she pointed out that part of the charm of a gift shop lay in its hodgepodge assortment of stock. People wanted to browse without feeling that someone was pressuring them to buy. As for the ones who wanted help, Lottie told her that the thing to do was to show what was interesting or unusual about the items on display.

No sooner had Holly taken off her coat and hat and turned on the different lamps that lighted the shop than two women came in looking for period dolls. Although she showed them all those on hand, not one in Lottie's large collection seemed to be exactly what they had in mind. But she did get them to sign their names in the register so Lottie would have a record for future mailings. You never could tell, she kept repeating, when lookers would pay off.

After they left, Holly went into a cubbyhole that opened out of the shop to type up the address labels for that day's mail orders. She was just starting when the doorbell jingled again.

"Charley!" A man's voice called out.

"There's no Charley here," Holly announced. Coming to the doorway of the little office, she looked across the room to see the conservation officer who had reprimanded her. The very sight of him made her cheeks burn with remembered embarrassment.

"Last I heard Charlotte Blaine still owned this place," he observed.

So Lottie was Charley to this man. "She still does," Holly answered. "If you want to see her, she's over at the town hall, up the street from here, working on the art show. There's a sign out front, so you can't miss it."

Through the window Holly watched him drive off in his black roadster. Thank goodness he hadn't remembered her. What, she wondered, could he want with Lottie? He must know her quite well, calling her by a nickname.

When, about an hour later, her employer returned with the conservationist, Holly pretended to ignore his presence. "Is everything ready for the show?" she asked.

Lottie nodded. "All the pictures are hung and the sculptures arranged. Craig helped the hanging committee. That's why we got through so soon." Then she indicated her companion. "I don't know if you two have met officially. Craig," she went on in her usual happy fashion, "may I present Holly Elliot? Holly, this is my cousin, Craig Wilmot."

"How do you do?" Holly managed to say. Only then did she realize what had been said. Cousin. The conservation officer was related to Lottie Blaine.

"I've asked Craig to stay to lunch," Lottie went on. "We'll have ourselves a little party."

Holly wasn't particularly intrigued by the prospect, but the meal, she knew, would be an interrupted affair. She got up to wait on the first person to arrive, soon after they sat down, and would have taken care of the second one also, but Lottie insisted that this time she would do it.

Alone with Craig Wilmot, Holly could think of nothing to say. But her companion quickly broke the silence.

[63]

"Unusually mild for December, isn't it?" he observed. "It's hard to realize Christmas is just three weeks off."

"Yes," she agreed.

His eyes were on her face. "I have a feeling I've met you before."

"You have," Holly told him.

He looked interested. "Where?"

"I'd rather not talk about it."

"Now you've aroused my curiosity."

Holly was silent.

"Could it have been when I was on duty?"

She nodded.

He snapped his fingers. "I recall now. Right off Goodhill Road. You were picking black alder."

"And you were perfectly horrid about it!"

He smiled self-consciously. "If I was, I apologize. I remember now that was the day I found car after car up on the back roads with people stripping the holly bushes. I guess I must have been pretty worked up. Why don't we cross it off the books and consider this our first meeting?"

Before she could reply, Lottie came back in. By this time Holly was feeling more at ease—now that the air had cleared. Actually, at close range, Craig Wilmot bore little resemblance to the ogre she had built up in her mind.

"How do you like living in the Housatonic Valley?" he asked now.

Lottie chuckled. "Careful how you answer that. Craig thinks there's no place on earth like this part of the country. Why do you know that for the past two summers he's spent his entire vacation canoeing from the headwaters of the

Housatonic, up above Pittsfield, Massachusetts, all the way down to Long Island Sound?"

"You make it sound as if I'm an eccentric or something," he objected.

"Aren't you?" teased his cousin.

"How long is the river?" Holly asked.

"About a hundred miles. But there are waterfalls and dams at intervals—which often means half a mile or more portage. Also there are a lot of side trips along the way—places like Arrowhead, in Pittsfield, the onetime farm home of Herman Melville, who wrote *Moby Dick*; and, in Lenox, the home of his friend Oliver Wendell Holmes. There's history all up and down the river."

Holly was about to make some remark, but he went on, "And did you know that, back in the days of the early settlers, the founding fathers of Milford carted with them what may have been the first prefabricated house in history?"

"No!" she laughed.

"I'm serious. From the New Haven Colony they brought along precut lengths of timber large enough to make a shelter and meeting house for the forty families. They did this so that each family would have a chance to put up a well-built house—almost an early attempt at zoning. Have you been to Milford?" he asked Holly.

"I don't even know where it is."

"Last town on our side of the river—the left bank—before it flows into the Sound. Even today many of the original houses are standing—which speaks well for the policy of the founding fathers."

For some time no one came into the shop. Now, at the

tinkle of the bell, Holly sprang gratefully to her feet. Very interesting, but she couldn't see why anyone would get all worked up over the Housatonic Valley. Now if it were Alaska she could understand—and that made her wonder if there would be a letter from Mark at home.

CHAPTER

8

The Sunday after Christmas and two days before Mark was due to arrive, Holly was in her room writing thank-you notes when she was interrupted by a knock on the door.

"Come in!" she called.

Hugh, who had shot up inches since last summer, came in carrying a pad and pencil. Recently he had acquired rimmed glasses, which were always slipping off the bridge of his nose and giving his face a rather quizzical expression.

"Want some help with your Christmas notes, brother?"

"Those!" He dismissed the subject with scorn. "Finished writing them all yesterday. I'm on important stuff now," and he held up the pad showing a long list of notations. "These are just a few of the people I still have to see or call. You're one of the ones I have to interview."

Holly couldn't hide her astonishment. "Interview me? What for?"

"I'm going to be editor of a paper. The *Goodhill Gazette*. Roy's circulation manager. He's out getting orders now. It's going to be five cents an issue and come out twice a month. Ads are fifty cents. I already have two—one from Miss Blaine and one from Mr. Fairchild. All I need are ten more," he added breathlessly.

Knowing Hugh's persuasiveness, Holly had no doubt that

he would get them; though of what benefit they would be to the advertisers, she couldn't see. "How are you going to print it?" she asked now. "With that set of hand-printing blocks you got a few years ago?"

"That kid stuff? I'm going to cut stencils on the typewriter and mimeograph it."

"On the school machine?"

"No. I'm buying my own."

"But they're too expensive!" In recent weeks she had looked into the matter, thinking it might be nice to have one to get out price lists and letters to mail-order customers; but they were much too high even with a weekly pay check.

"I already paid a deposit," Hugh informed her. "I'm getting a good deal—twenty dollars secondhand. I used my birthday money for the down payment, and I got ten for Christmas; and, counting the ads I already have, I only need four dollars more." He dismissed that as a matter of little account. "Now let's get down to the interview."

"But what do you want to interview me about?" Holly wanted to know.

He turned to a clean page on the pad, poised his pencil above it. "How does it feel to be in the mail-order business?"

"Hugh Elliot, you know very well I'm just starting in! Don't print this, but up to now I've had only three orders. If you're looking for a story, why don't you interview Lottie Blaine? She sells a lot by mail."

"She's not in the neighborhood."

"But you got an ad from her. Advertisers," she quoted, recalling her high-school journalism, "are entitled to a little free publicity."

The idea didn't catch her brother's fancy. "I want to do the mail-order story about you," he maintained.

"Why, Hugh, that's very sweet of you."

He passed this over with a gruff "Got to find somebody else on Goodhill Road for this issue."

"You could wait till Mark comes and have him give you a story on what you have to do to get ready for work with the weather bureau."

"But he doesn't live here now."

"He's a summer resident." Even as she said it, Holly hoped he would be working at the Fairchilds' again next summer. At least he hadn't said anything to the contrary. Hugh added Mark's name to his list and left, saying he had to make some more phone calls and would do the interview later.

Pen in hand, Holly stared meditatively off across the still snowless countryside. It wasn't a Christmasy landscape at all, with the gray, bare trees pointing bony fingers skyward. It had turned very cold, too, and everything stood out bleak and sharp without the softening touch of haze that had marked the warmer days. There was an almost unreal quality to everything, but once Mark came she knew everything would be different. Then, right in the midst of these thoughts, she became aware of voices across the hall.

"One thing is certain, young man," she heard her father saying. "I won't have you start out half-cocked on this newspaper venture. If you begin, see it through; but before you launch the project, make sure you're really set. Which brings me to another question—do you have the money for your supplies?"

"You mean the mimeograph paper? I'm going to sell more ads," she could hear Hugh reply.

"You can't count on that. Besides, that should be considered future income. And had you figured on ink and stencils?"

"I thought they came with the machine," admitted her brother just as Holly hurried over to referee the bout between the two.

"I'll buy the supplies," she announced.

"Why should you?" demanded their father. "That's hardly good training for Hugh. If he needs more money, he should go out and scratch for it himself."

"But he can help me out too." The idea had just occurred to her. "I'm going to need lots of mimeographing done for my mail orders. Instead of taking it to a public stenographer or sending it to a mail-mimeographing place, Hugh could take care of it for me. How would you like to be my job printer, Hugh?" she asked.

"Sure, Hol." His gratitude was evident.

"I'd cut the stencils on the typewriter. Then all you'd have to do would be to run them off. We can figure out how much each job is worth. When you've caught up to what you owe me for supplies, I'll pay you for each piece of work you do."

Their father got up from the homespun-covered studio couch on which he had been sitting, "Well, think I'll leave you two to thrash out the details. As long as you can both make a satisfactory deal, it's all right with me." He yawned, smiled apologetically. "Think I'll go catch forty winks. Haven't recovered from the Christmas festivities yet."

They both listened to his footsteps receding down the hall, then going down the stairs to his study. Hugh gave her a conspiratorial look. "Thanks a lot, Hol."

"Look, I really meant it about your doing work for me!"

He was on the defensive. "I didn't say I wouldn't."

"Well, just so you don't forget."

Now, as she sat here, another idea came to her. Ever since the HOLLY LOVES MARK episode, the spatter stencil set had been taking up space in her room. She had made several attempts to return it, but each time she found it back on her table. Hugh would have none of it. The other day Lottie Blaine had suggested that she order imprinted stationery for answering mail-order inquiries. That, too, involved more money than she could spare right now. But a piece of advertising mail that had reached her on Christmas Eve had a spatter-stenciled letterhead which was also repeated on the back of the envelope. It looked attractive and eye-catching. Using the same method, she could design something for herself.

In the latest issue of *Home Handcrafter* she had read that shopkeepers who sold across the counter had their store surroundings to impress the personality of their business on their shoppers, but all the mail-order person had, to put himself across, was his mail. The more imagination and individuality displayed on envelopes, mailing pieces, and stickers, the more likely people would be to remember what you had to offer. Now she proposed to Hugh that she buy back the stencil set.

He looked embarrassed. "You can have it."

"It will be two dollars more toward your mimeograph

machine," she urged, and her brother was too good a businessman to say "No" to that.

Going back to her room, Holly sat down to write more thank-you notes. When she finished, the early winter twilight had set in. As she started downstairs, she could see that the door to her parents' room was closed—which meant her mother was resting. In the study her father was just waking up from his nap.

"Holly," he called, "come in here a minute."

"Yes, Dad."

He patted the chair beside the couch on which he was lying. "Sit down, darling."

She complied, wondering what he had on his mind.

"Mother and I have been rather worried about you."

"Worried—about me?" she echoed, and added, "Why?" But she was sure she knew what the answer would be. Mark's impending visit. That was what had brought this on. Even though she hadn't come out and said in so many words that they planned to marry as soon as Mark was graduated, they must surely know how she felt about him.

But when her father spoke, he didn't mention Mark's name at all.

"How serious are you about this mail-order business?" he wanted to know.

"Oh!" There was startled relief in her tone. "Very much so. That's why I'm working at Lottie's gift shop—to get money for more ads, and materials for making things to sell."

"I gathered that. But your mother and I feel responsible for your change in plan. If we weren't living out here so far away from transportation facilities, you would have gone ahead with your original idea of learning to become a buyer. We're afraid it's the location that's influenced you."

Holly was quick with her answer. "No, Dad, it isn't! I never realized the possibilities in mail order till I met Mr. Ames and Lottie, and began to correspond with the editors of *Hodgepodge*. All my life, wherever I live—even when I'm married—I can sell the things I make by mail, and be my own boss." She was tempted to add, "Even if I live in Alaska"; but she didn't quite dare.

"And what guarantee do you have that you can make a financial go of it? I was reading an article the other day that said twenty per cent of all small businesses—both those that had started with a shoestring capital and those with a generous budget—failed in the first two years, and that includes mail order too."

"Mine won't, once I really get it started."

"Holly, it takes more than determination to succeed."

"I'm learning a lot from Lottie's mail-order work and the mail-order magazines I take."

"Maybe so. But if I were going into a certain field, I'd want to be as completely informed as possible. Everybody knows about the two big general mail-order houses that have built up to a tremendous success over the years—Sears Roebuck and Montgomery Ward. Judging by the circulars and catalogues that come by mail, there are a large number of retail stores that run a mail-order business on the side. There also seem to be a goodly number of concerns that specialize in offering gifts and gadgets to the public. But how do small independents like yourself become established?"

"By advertising."

"Earrings wouldn't tempt me."

"Not even for mother?" Holly wanted to know.

"I'd go to a department store or a jeweler for them—not send somewhere by mail."

"I'm just trying to get women interested in my earrings and handbags."

"Don't you think you would increase your potential market if you offered things that both men and women would buy—or added something that women would buy for men, like the plaid wool muffler with the yarn fringe you made me for Christmas?"

"That is a good idea, Dad; but I couldn't get in an ad on that before February or March, and that would be too late for a winter item."

"What are some of the things other people advertise in those magazines of yours?"

"Oh, raw materials like mill-end pieces of fabrics, felt, netting, ribbons and laces at special prices, buttons, jewelry findings—"

"What are findings?" her father interrupted.

"Accessories you need for jewelry work—jump rings, catches, pin backs, ear screws of different kinds, and so on."

"I see."

"Quite a few people seem to go in for dolls or doll hospitals or dressmaking for dolls. Others make greeting cards to order; do textile painting on towels, tablecloths, and clothes; raise plants like cacti to sell; do ceramics; make baby bibs, bootees, sweaters, and children's wear." Holly paused for breath and made a quick mental review of some of the other ads she had seen in the latest issue of *Hodgepodge*. "Some specialize in aprons or hankies," she went on. "Others go in for toys, or patterns and directions for making things, or jewelry of all kinds. Some sell gadgets like sardine servers, different doorbells or knockers, salt and pepper sets, and other items they import or buy from makers in this country." She half rose. "Want me to get the magazine and read you some of the others?"

"I'll take your word that there's plenty of variety. Also you seem to be quite well informed on the woman-doing-hand-work-at-home-to-sell-by-mail side of the field. But the other day at the library I went through the card catalogue and discovered that there have been quite a few books written on mail order. I'm sure you could get some pointers from the case histories and stories of people who have made a success in the field."

"Why didn't you bring some home?"

He smiled. "After all, darling, I didn't want to cram them down your throat—just thought I'd call them to your attention and you could get them if you wanted to."

"I'd like them." Now that she was no longer faced with compulsory reading for classes, she enjoyed books of special interest like the ones on Alaska. Seeing what there was on mail order would be fun too. "What library were the books in?" she added.

"Waterbury. I can drive you over any afternoon this week when you're through at Miss Blaine's."

"Tomorrow?"

"Fine." He sat up. "Mother and I were feeling guilty, but I'm glad to see you so enthusiastic."

It was true—the mail-order field intrigued her, and she

was not minimizing how much it meant in her romantic scheme of things. She had rather thought her father and her mother might have put two and two together; but since they hadn't, there was no need to bring it up herself right now.

After supper the evening stretched ahead, long and lonesome without Mark. Now that his coming was not far off, each minute seemed to drag. Then the phone rang and it was Alice to say that the ice on the lake was perfect for skating and wouldn't they all like to come down. A cozy evening by the fire seemed more attractive to her parents, but Holly and the boys headed for Azalea Acres.

When they reached the brow of the hill behind the Fairchilds' house, the lake was already alive with motion. From up here, with searchlights strung up in some of the trees bordering it, the scene looked like something out of a Hollywood dream sequence. To make the illusion complete, someone had started a record on the terrace overlooking the ice— and the skaters were waltzing to Tchaikovsky's "Sleeping Beauty." The boys plunged down the hill, eager to begin skating as soon as possible; but Holly remained where she was, to enjoy the panorama. The happy laughter and calls of the skaters, the sound of the blades singing over the ice, the mood-evoking waltz, and the wood-smoke-scented air from the crackling blaze in the barbecue fireplace—all underlined her anticipation.

Sitting on a bench near the edge of the sloping bank as she put on her skates, Holly saw familiar faces swirl past— coming out of shadow into the beam of the searchlights. The Fairchilds were on skates, and so were Lottie and Craig Wilmot. She hadn't expected to see them there. From her vantage point she also watched her brothers hurry down the other side of the pond and disappear into the melee of skaters. Then, ready herself, she started down the bank. But she hadn't quite remembered how steep it was. She tried to dig in with her skates for footing, but the ground was frozen too hard. The next thing she knew she was losing her balance and having the nightmarish sensation of painfully sliding along the ice on her hands and knees while skaters swerved sharply to avoid her.

"Are you hurt?" a voice called out almost before she came to a stop, and then Craig Wilmot was bending over her.

"I'm all right," she told him. But even through her Swedish mittens the palms of her hands burned and she could feel her knees bleeding. She tried to get up, but she felt numb from the shock of the fall. Clem Fairchild had come over and now an ever-growing circle surrounded her.

"I'll be all right," Holly insisted again. She hated to make a spectacle of herself. And it wasn't as though she wasn't a good skater. The two winters they had lived in Michigan, when Mother and Dad had taught there, she had spent most of her after-school hours and practically every week end on the ice.

In spite of her protests Mr. Fairchild and Craig, with Alice Fairchild running ahead, helped her up to the house for first aid.

"I'm sorry to be such a bother," she apologized when she was seated in the kitchen.

"It's no bother. We're just sorry you can't join in the skating tonight," her hostess remarked as she wrung out a cloth in hot water and sponged Holly's cuts.

Presently, disinfected and bandaged, she was seated in a comfortable chair in the living room before one of the full-length windows that gave a view of the lake and the skaters below. "You're going down again, aren't you?" she asked the others.

"I was coming back anyhow to make some hot chocolate," Alice told her. "Clem, why don't you go see who's going to join us."

"What can I do to make myself useful?" Craig wanted to know.

"You can get cups and saucers down out of the cabinet for me. Then you can keep Holly company."

Alone, Holly drew a deep, exasperated breath. What a thing to happen to her just a few days before Mark came! The way she had barked her knees, she would probably be too stiff even to dance this week, and Mark loved dancing. Out in the kitchen she could hear the clatter of china, and Lottie's cousin talking to Alice. She knew tonight's happening wasn't his fault, but it seemed that Craig Wilmot's presence always spelled trouble for her. Outside, the skaters seemed to be having a wonderful time. Looking down on them made her so envious of the fun she was missing that she got up and made her way to another chair, away from the window.

It was then that Craig joined her. "How do you feel now?"

"Better, thanks," she told him. But as far as her state of mind went, she felt worse. "I would have to be a spoilsport!" she added.

"It happens in the best of families," he said.

Holly hadn't expected such a flip remark and, in her

present mood, it provoked her. Groping about for some way to get a rise out of him, she said with calm deliberation, "I'm surprised you weren't on the Housatonic tonight."

"Not frozen," he commented. "Besides, I like the valley as much as I do the river itself—and this countryside is all part of it."

"You can have it!"

Surprised, he looked at her. "You don't like it?"

She shook her head. "It's horribly dull!"

This time she drew sparks. "And what do you consider the ideal spot in which to live?" he wanted to know.

"Alaska." She spoke it triumphantly.

"Oh? Why Alaska?"

She was tempted to tell him about Mark, but didn't. "It has so much to offer—adventure, opportunities for work and fun, spectacular scenery, all kinds of exciting things."

"I'll match you point for point along the Housatonic," he maintained just as Lottie came bouncing in to join them.

"Do I hear *that* word again?" she laughed.

She was followed by some of the other skaters, including Hugh and Roy, and the conversation became general. Holly couldn't help noticing that Hugh had pulled out his little pad and was making notes. When they were called into the dining room for refreshments, he hurried over to her.

"Thanks for giving me a story, Hol," he told her in a low voice.

"Hugh Elliot, you're not going to write about my fall!"

"It's news, isn't it?"

"You want your supplies, don't you?"

But he came back at her with, "If you want me to do

[79]

work for you, you can't censor the press," and she could make no further protest.

By and by her parents came to get the boys, because it was way past their bedtime. When the Fairchilds offered to drive Holly up later, Craig said he and Lottie could drop her off; so the impromptu party continued. After second servings of hot chocolate accompanied by more Christmas cookies and fruitcake, they all went back to the living room. They were talking and watching a TV show, Craig Wilmot sitting at her feet because there weren't enough chairs to go round, when the doorbell rang.

"Wonder who that can be," observed Clem Fairchild, going to answer it.

Framed in the doorway, when he opened it, stood Mark.

CHAPTER

9

"That was a cozy little scene, if anyone should ask!" Mark's tone as he drove Holly up the hill was bitter. Since his unexpected arrival, he hadn't had too much to say; but now he was making up for it. "I don't think you were even glad to see me!"

"Why, Mark, what a thing to say!" Holly found it hard to keep the hurt out of her voice. "I was so surprised I didn't know what to say."

"And you didn't want to let on that you knew me!"

"Mark, what's the matter with you?"

"How would you feel if you were me and you thought you were going to surprise your girl early the next day by dropping over to her house, and then you find her at a party with another guy sitting at her feet acting as though she were his property!"

"Mark!" She couldn't keep the exasperation out of her tone. "Craig Wilmot means nothing to me."

"No? Well, that's not the way it looked from where I sat. He had his eyes on you all evening. Why did he insist he was going to drive you home?"

"*With* his cousin, Lottie Blaine," she reminded him. "He

had told the Fairchilds he would—before you came—so they wouldn't have to bother. He was just being polite."

"Hmmm!" Mark still sounded disgruntled. "It's a wonder I got to drive you home at all!"

By now they had reached the professor's house, but instead of stopping he continued slowly up the road. "If you knew how crazy I've been to see you! Even Thanksgiving day, after coming all the way down, I couldn't have a couple of hours with you. Then I got to thinking why didn't I get down a few days earlier—I knew the Fairchilds wouldn't mind—and here I am."

"Hello," said Holly.

"Hello yourself," he chuckled, then added, "Do you have to sit quite so far away?"

Lottie called early the next morning to say not to bother coming over to the shop if she didn't feel up to it. Things should be pretty quiet anyhow today, she added. Holly wondered if she suspected she would like to spend the time with Mark; but if that was in the back of Lottie's mind, she didn't say so.

Soon after breakfast Mark arrived and her father and mother drew him out about college. Watching them, Holly thought what a bombshell she could throw into the placid conversation by saying, "Do you realize it's your future son-in-law you're talking to?" But there was no need to put it into words because Mark still had another two years at M.I.T. Then Roy catapulted into the room to show off Misty, who was now almost full-grown, and Hugh came in, impatient to tell of his newspaper venture. Before they knew it, it was noon and time for lunch. After that, Alice Fairchild phoned to ask if Holly and Mark would have dinner with them. They needn't, she was quick to add, feel they had to stay around all evening.

The rest of the afternoon seemed to pass in a rush. Just a short while after Alice's call, it seemed, they were sitting at a candlelit table with her and Clem, and discussing the annual business-vacation trip the Fairchilds would soon be making to Florida.

"Have you heard about Holly's work in mail order?" Mrs. Fairchild asked Mark when the conversation became too one-sided.

He looked surprised. "All I know about is her job at the gift shop."

"Tell him, Holly," Alice Fairchild urged.

"There isn't much to tell yet," she said. "I barely have a toehold." She appreciated Mrs. Fairchild's wanting to play up what she was doing, but she hadn't thought to caution her that she wanted to wait to tell Mark until she had some real success.

Clem Fairchild, whom she had by now discovered to be an extraordinarily perceptive person, seemed to sense her unwillingness to talk about it and at once introduced another subject.

"You'll be glad to hear that the state is growing more and more conservation-minded," he told Mark. "That young chap you met last night, Craig Wilmot, is one of the field men. Doing a good job too."

Holly realized that, as far as Mark was concerned, this was an unfortunate choice of topic. But he parried it adroitly.

[83]

"The place where the government has a real conservation problem on its hands is Alaska," he said, and proceeded to elaborate on the reindeer situation.

"What about natural resources?" Alice Fairchild inquired during dessert.

"There are still plenty of those, like great untapped coal mines," Mark told her. "You can find pretty much anything you want in Alaska. In many places the country is still untouched. The big problem is how to haul things in quantity unless you're on a waterway, the railroad, or a highway. Thousands and thousands of square miles are still completely uninhabited. People who want to homestead can certainly have their pick."

"I like the country, but I'd want neighbors," Alice Fairchild put in.

Out in the hall a clock struck the half-hour. "My goodness! If you two are going to the movies, you'll have to hurry."

A short while later they were heading down the hill in the station wagon.

"Do you really want to go to the movies?" This time it was Mark who asked the question.

Holly shook her head. "No. I'd rather drive and talk." Outside of late last night, they had scarcely been alone to catch up on things.

"I know just the drive," Mark told her. "Roxbury by moonlight."

A short while later they turned left off the main street of Woodbury and headed out into a moonlight-washed landscape where white colonial houses, illuminated upstairs and down, showed off the cozy, comfortably furnished interiors.

"What's with this mail order?" Mark asked suddenly. "Why haven't you told me about it?"

"I wanted to surprise you once it was going well."

"Why are you fooling around with it?"

Holly couldn't conceal her indignation. "I'd hardly call it fooling! I've been working hard in my spare time making earrings and handbags and answering inquiries."

"I didn't mean it the way it sounded. I know you must have been working hard. But why?"

"So that I would have something to do that would bring in money wherever I lived."

"If you mean Alaska, in the first place I'm the one who supports the family. In the second place you'll be much too busy there for that sort of thing."

"Why?" she challenged.

They had reached a rise in the road and now Mark pulled off to the side so that they had a widespread view of the countryside below. "I've decided," he told her, "that we're going to be homesteaders. With so much fine land there just for the taking—a hundred and sixty acres for filing a five-dollar claim—we'd be fools not to do it instead of waiting for me to get a job with the weather bureau in a place like Anchorage, where there'd be too many people around. That way we could live off the land and leave a lot of the headaches of civilization behind—like utility bills and insurance. We'll go native, eat game and fish, maybe even raise our own grain and grind it for bread—after we build our cabin."

Holly had listened in stunned silence, a million questions

running through her mind. Now she recovered sufficiently to say, "But that sort of life would take all our time."

"Who cares?"

She was tempted to cry out that she did. Instead, as if she didn't already know, she asked him when he thought of leaving. His answer was another shock.

"End of this semester. Soon as I take my final exams, we'll get married and go."

To Holly it seemed that the conversation had taken on the dimensions of a nightmare. "Do your parents know about your plans?" she inquired now.

"Why get them all worked up? My father has his heart set on my getting a scientific degree. He made out fine without one—he's earned a lot more money than many guys with degrees, and he knows just as much if not more."

"And your mother?" she prodded him.

"She lives in a world of her own—clubs and antiques. Been a better thing for her if my father hadn't made so much money—if she'd had to do her own work and had raised a big family instead of just having me."

"But what would she think of your going?" Holly insisted.

"The best way to save a fuss would be to act first, let them know afterward. We could elope, then send our folks a wire from Alaska."

"Mark"—her voice reflected her anger—"I happen to love my family and I don't want to do anything behind their backs. Besides, I think you should finish college the way your father wants you to—and be set for a job in the weather bureau even if you don't take one right away."

"I'm through. Fed up! This winter is the time for us to make the break."

"Well, I'm not ready to make the break. I was counting on another two years to get used to the idea of Alaska. I'm trying to build up a mail-order business, not only as a source of income but as a means of communication—contact with the rest of the world. I can't drop it just like that, when I've begun to put so much into it."

"But I told you before—living off the land is going to take all our time. And don't think we'll have regular mail service even if you did manage to make things. The nearest settlement or neighbor might be twenty, fifty, or a hundred miles off. If we were lucky, a bush pilot might fly in now and again with mail and a few staples we just couldn't do without."

A vision of the cozy, well-kept homes they had driven by rose up before her. "Mark, we don't have to live that way," she told him.

"I want to."

"But I don't!" The words were out before she even knew she had said them.

"Don't you love me?" he asked.

"If you loved me you'd consider what I wanted to do too," she countered.

"I thought you liked the idea of living in Alaska!"

"But homesteading—" She let the sentence dangle in midair. She had read enough books on living in the wilds of Alaska to know she would not be happy under primitive conditions. Escape to the Territory had seemed so romantic! In some unaccountable way Mark had changed; it was almost as though he were a stranger. Or was it that suddenly she was seeing him for the self-centered, selfish boy he was? Was she in love with him or had she been in love with the idea of the new life Alaska had offered? Her thoughts were a confused whirl.

"Please, Mark, let's not talk about it any more tonight. Take me home."

"Okay, anything you say." Already he was turning the station wagon around.

Lying awake that night, Holly found all the things she hadn't been able to say or think come rushing fluently into her consciousness. "You don't want a partner—a wife," she would tell him tomorrow. "What you want is a squaw woman—a docile creature who will agree with everything you want, do everything you say, and work hard in the house and out in the fields beside you. Well, you can keep your old grain-grinding and the rest of it! I'm a person in my own right too. I have special desires and dreams, too, and you're not going to come between me and them!" Then, with an eloquent gesture, she would hand him back his identification bracelet. Yet, deep down, she had the feeling that she and Mark had to do a lot more talking—maybe she could make him change his mind after all.

The following morning after breakfast Hugh came in carrying a large envelope. "For you, Hol," he announced. "Funny thing, it was in the mailbox without any stamps. I wonder who put it there?"

Holly's heart was hammering. Already she knew. "Give it to me, Hugh!" she cried, and hurried from the kitchen up to her own room. Through the envelope she could feel a

[88]

familiar shape. As she tore open one end, her own bracelet fell out and with it a note.

Dear Miss Sears & Roebuck:

It was nice knowing you. Sorry I didn't know sooner I was competing with Big Business. One of these years when you've developed a set of ulcers and sit counting your millions, think of me by a campfire, before my cabin in the wild, happly gnawing a hunk of venison with not a care in the world. Since we both said all there was to say last night, there is no point in rehashing it again. By the time you receive this, I shall be on my way.

MARK

Holly read and reread the letter in stunned silence. So there was no more to say! It was all over, just like that! She tore the letter into shreds. "Miss Sears & Roebuck . . . Big Business"—well, that did it!

If she had had any ideas of not keeping on with mail order, the memory of this stinging note was all the incentive she needed. She would create a mail-order business that would be known from coast to coast. Even in Alaska, Mark would hear of her. Ironically it had been with the idea of her life and Mark's in Alaska that she had begun mail order. Now for a very different reason she would carry on. And one of these years Mr. Mark Logan was going to be very sorry for the way he had acted and sounded off!

CHAPTER

10

CONSERVATION MAN ANSWERS SOME QUESTIONS

Mr. Craig Wilmot, a state conservation officer, well known to many residents of Goodhill Road, spoke to this reporter about some of the problems the state department of conservation is working on.

Besides conserving precious natural resources like soil and water and replanting natural growths like trees, Mr. Wilmot suggests that people go out of their way to preserve rare birds and game and plants. As a case of thoughtlessness, he told about a patch of fringed gentians growing on the edge of a field owned by Mr. and Mrs. Clement Fairchild of Goodhill Road. They were the largest stand of these rare wild flowers left in the state. Last fall some motorists gathered them by the armful, leaving only a few small plants. This spring none have come up.

Craig Wilmot graduated with a B.S. from the University of Connecticut. He also did graduate work at Cornell University in Ithaca, New York. Before working in Connecticut, he was employed by the New York

State Department of Agriculture, then was with the Connecticut State Experimental Station before taking up his present work.

Holly put down the late May issue of the *Goodhill Gazette*, which now came out regularly every second Saturday. Just because Craig Wilmot considered his conservation work a thing of great importance didn't mean that other people had to get excited about it. Of course her brother Hugh was always on the lookout for something to take up space, so she couldn't really blame him.

The little mimeographed newspaper was doing very well, much better than her mail order. Hugh and Roy between them had managed to sign up over fifty families which took in not only the residents along Goodhill Road but also those of adjacent Quaker Farms and Southbury, important to her because it had the nearest post office. Besides what Hugh took in on subscriptions, he now had sixteen advertisers—which gave him eight dollars each issue for ads alone. If it hadn't been for her job at the gift shop, she would have had to borrow from him to pay for the space she was taking in different magazines. Not too many people ordered the dollar earrings and two-dollar handbags which were featured in the ads, but an increasing number were writing in for the free price list which Hugh mimeographed for her. With a choice of ten articles, she had hoped that when people did order they would select two or three; but invariably the coins or stamps were usually for just one low-priced item. It was very discouraging.

"Remember, you're competing with established stores,"

Lottie had told her the other day. "The dollar earrings you advertise are very nice and well worth the price, but it would take a color reproduction to do them justice."

To pay someone for making even a simple line drawing and have it reproduced by an engraver in a plate which would come out black and white was more than she could afford right now. "You mean people hate to buy a pig in a poke?" she asked.

"There's something to that, Holly. Also there's price appeal. I don't mean the handbags—they're certainly reasonable enough; but when you can go to a store and select nice mass-produced earrings for a dollar, you aren't going to the trouble of writing out an order, addressing and stamping an envelope, and perhaps even paying for a money order or check. If you sold for a lower price, you might have more of a chance."

"But I wouldn't be making so much on each pair of earrings."

"You'd be making more sales though."

"Then why don't I have more takers for my quarter earrings?"

"Perhaps too many people know how to make simple button earrings. Practically every dime store and button counter sell ear backs, and household cement is easy to come by."

"You mean I need something more unique?"

"Or at least some earrings different from what anyone else is offering."

But what kind? That was the question. Well, she was going to keep on experimenting until she did come up with something new. She was determined to show her father that she wasn't a job butterfly—that she could stick with something and make a go of it. Equally powerful was the drive to let Mark see that she could make a big success of mail order. Sooner or later the Fairchilds would get the word to him.

Even as she thought of Mark, her eyes fell on yet another headline in the *Goodhill Gazette*.

FORMER SUMMER RESIDENT GOES TO ALASKA

Mr. Mark Logan, formerly gardener and assistant to Mr. and Mrs. Clement Fairchild, recently flew to Alaska, where he will live. Using Fairbanks as his headquarters, Mr. Logan will explore the surrounding territory until he finds a suitable homesteading site.

Holly knew where Hugh had obtained that little item. Alice Fairchild had shown her a letter Mark had written. If she was aware that there had been a serious romance between the two of them, she gave no sign. What reason he had given for his early departure during the holidays Holly would never know. All Alice had said was "Too bad Mark couldn't have stayed longer," and had dropped the subject.

Now, almost five months later, she could recall the incident with a detached air. Her mother came into her room and she felt suddenly confidential.

"Did you see this about Mark?" she asked, tapping the news with her finger.

"Yes, I did, dear."

Holly took a self-conscious turn around the room. "You

[93]

didn't know, did you, that Mark wanted me to go to Alaska with him?"

Her mother shook her head, then added, "But Dad and I realized you were quite serious about him."

"How did you feel about it?"

"Not too happy."

"Then why didn't you say something?"

"And make him seem more desirable?"

"But how were you able to keep quiet?" she persisted.

Her mother smiled. "Don't think it wasn't hard. We didn't have anything against Mark, you understand. We just didn't think he was the boy for you."

"Perhaps it was proximity."

"Maybe so, darling." She rose. "Well, I'd better be getting back to the dinner. And thanks for telling me."

"I wanted to. I'll be down to help right away."

Brushing her hair, Holly was glad she had come out with it at last. Oddly, Mark had helped her more than he knew. Though she had never admitted it to anyone, all through high school she had lived in a private state of panic that no boy would ever ask her to marry him. She recalled that one of her aunts had once said, "Any girl can get married. The trick is to marry the right man." Now that someone had asked her, she no longer felt insecure about her ability to awaken romantic dreams. But, if she was going to make Mark Logan regret his sarcastic words, she would have to attend strictly to business for some time to come.

"Good issue you brought out, Hugh," commented their father at dinner.

"Thanks, Dad."

"Don't forget I helped staple the paper and deliver it," Roy reminded him.

"You're doing a fine job too," he smiled, then turned to Holly. "Read something this afternoon that will interest you."

"What, Dad?"

"Seems there's a young man in Connecticut who is making quite a thing out of manufacturing and selling bird calls by mail. They've even been adopted as the official Aubudon bird call."

"Did it say how long he's been in business?"

"Only about a year and a half. He's doing so well he even has a sales manager in England."

"How did he get started?"

"You'll want to read the newspaper article yourself. I've saved it. He became acquainted with a professional bird hunter in Italy. He brought back some of the whistles and worked out his own design. Now his idea is patented. Seems you can imitate the call of almost any bird with it."

"Can I have one?" asked Roy. "I'd sure like to fool the birds."

"Think I'd like one too," Hugh put in.

"Look, you young financier," Walter Elliot chuckled. "You can afford to buy your own. Besides, they're not expensive. What was interesting to me," he added, turning back to Holly, "is that he developed something that has no competition. Also, as you can see by the reaction here, it holds a tremendous appeal for families with children as well as for bird watchers. The market is practically unlimited."

An unlimited market. That's what she was hoping for too.

But how to achieve it? The dishes done, Holly took the latest issue of *Hodgepodge* under her arm and started down the road. It had rained earlier in the afternoon, but since then the sun had burned its way through the mists. A moist, fragrant steaminess distilled of tender young grass, flowering shrubs, and spring flowers now filled the air. Passing the Fairchilds' place, she could see the wild azaleas, like pink tinted balls of popcorn, dotting the hillsides.

So much had happened that it was hard to realize she and her family had already been here eleven months. Holly shifted the magazine to her other arm. Considering Hugh's success, and the success of clearing-house publications like *Hodgepodge*, which was run by two homemakers, she was tempted to start a magazine of her own. She would offer space, both display and classified, at reasonable rates to people who created handmades or to suppliers. Readers could enjoy armchair shopping. Advertisers like herself were happy to see ads listing raw materials at less than store prices, or hard-to-find materials. Gift shops listed their wants from craftsmen—creations they wanted to handle on consignment or to buy outright. Then there were chatty letters from the editors, special news from readers, how-to articles, and often success stories. But compiling even a small magazine would keep her pretty well glued to a typewriter when she would rather be making things with her hands.

Taking the side road that branched off to Jackson's Cove, Holly wished she could come up with something as good as the bird whistle. How, she wondered, did one dream up something that was different and exclusive? The trouble was she didn't even have a catchy name for her mail-order enterprise. The *Handcrafter* was colorless.

At the deserted cove she sat down on a rock, conscious that the air was dank and cool with a mingled smell of woods and river. Opening her *Hodgepodge* magazine, she began leafing through it. And there, right in the center spread, smiling up at her, almost as though he could see her, was the photograph of a very nice-looking young man sitting behind a table on which were displayed a variety of ceramics including period-doll parts. Both photograph and the accompanying text were reproduced from a Florida paper.

TALENTED YOUNG CERAMICS DESIGNER OPENS LARGER STUDIO

Duncan Moore, ceramics designer, whose work has already aroused much favorable comment in Florida, moved this week to a larger studio which will enable him to take care of the many orders by mail which come to him from all over the United States and Canada. Mr. Moore's mail-order business came into being by accident, he told this reporter, when out-of-staters who had visited his studio and bought his unusual vases, candlesticks, and table centerpieces with raised marine motifs, so realistic they look natural, wrote and ordered further pieces for relatives and friends.

Holly sighed. Two success stories in one day! Imagine having a mail-order business practically fall into your lap. Unfortunately she had neither a studio nor a shop. Even if they had had the room, the family's present location, so far from the main highways, was an obstacle. Of course she was learning a lot about the gift-shop business from Lottie, and by the summer's end, when the professor came back, the family might be moving to a more-traveled location. At least she hoped so.

On the right-hand side of the spread was a large ad featuring the Duncan Moore ceramics studio with photographic reproductions of the items offered for sale. She was about to turn the page when her eye fell on the price opposite the period-doll parts. Three dollars. Why didn't she order a few heads with matching limbs; make the rag torsos, dress them, and, at seven or eight dollars, add them to her offerings? She—

"Hello, there!" sang out a voice.

Holly had started at the sound. Now she stared in disbelief, with a feeling of this-is-where-I-came-in, as a dinghy with a figure came gliding into the cove. Then as the bow grated on the gravelly bottom, she realized her memory had been playing tricks on her. This wasn't Mark. This was another resident of Goodhill Road, a well-known artist about her father's age who lived with his wife in a small, old-fashioned house north of Azalea Acres and painted in the big barn behind it.

"Hello, Mr. Early," she greeted him.

"How are you, Holly?"

"Fine, thanks. Any luck fishing?" she added.

"Better than I expected."

Half seeing, she watched Dana Early fasten his boat; pick up the oars, his fishing gear and pail.

"Can I help you?" she heard herself saying even as on that earlier occasion.

He gave her a genial smile. "Thanks very much, but I can manage," he told her, jumping ashore. "Glad I ran into you. Saves trying to reach you by phone. My wife and I are giving a studio party two weeks from tonight—Saturday. Supper and square dancing. We want you to come and bring a boy friend if you'd like."

All the way home Holly thought about the invitation. Square dancing would be fun. But how could she possibly go without an escort?

CHAPTER

11

Dear Holly Elliot:

Many thanks for your order. The doll parts go out to you parcel post, special handling in this afternoon's mail. Yours is the first mail order for the dolls, which I have only recently started making. If it isn't too much trouble, I would like to see a photograph of the completed and dressed dolls. Should it be something I can use in my ads, I shall be glad to pay you.

Cordially yours,

DUNCAN MOORE

Holly was so excited over the warm friendliness of the letter that she took it to the shop to show Lottie.

"He needn't have told me mine was his first order," she beamed. "I'm beginning to think you meet some pretty nice people by mail."

In the literature that accompanied the letter, there had been a picture of him. He looked even better than in the newspaper photo, she thought—nice eyes; dark and wavy hair; a sensitive, fine-boned face; tapering, artistic fingers. As for his clothes, they might have come straight out of an ad in *Esquire*. The article about him reprinted in *Hodgepodge* had said he lived alone with a Great Dane. Why did a person like Duncan Moore have to be way off in Sarasota?

She became conscious that Lottie was speaking. "Don't think," she chuckled, "that you're the only one who has contacts by mail. I'm having a luncheon date today with a man I've never seen."

For the first time Holly grew aware that her friend was wearing a lovely new pastel print frock and very high-heeled shoes. She had been so preoccupied with her own affairs and problems that it had been a long while since she had looked at Lottie appraisingly. With her pretty vivaciousness she could have been a fashion or photographer's model.

"Who is he and why? Tell me all," she demanded.

Lottie began dusting some of the china figurines. "It's nothing exciting really—a customer from Chicago who just happens to be driving through today. He's looking for a location for a clock museum. After seeing a picture of this place in one of the ads, he said he'd like to buy it."

Holly's eyes widened. "And are you going to sell?"

But Lottie's "Heavens, no!" was reassuring.

"Why are you going out with him then?" she asked, before she realized how tactless the remark was.

But Lottie took it in good grace. "Maybe just for the dickens," she told her airily. "It's been a long, long winter."

At Holly's expression, Lottie laughed again. "Don't look at me as though you thought I were going to elope or something. All I'm going to do is have lunch with the man, say good-by, and come back to the shop. I'd like to see you kick over the traces once in a while yourself. What you do here would be enough, but then you have all that mail-order work at home."

"I'm going to a party next Saturday," Holly informed her. "A big one at Mr. Early's studio."

"Good!"

Holly was tempted to say she could bring an escort but had no idea whom to ask when the doorbell tinkled and a short, balding little man walked in.

"Are you Mrs. Blaine?" he inquired. "I'm Mr. Weatherby."

Holly extended a hand in Lottie's direction. "That's Mrs. Blaine."

After the two had left, with Lottie pausing in the doorway to roll her eyes in an expression of comic despair, Holly continued with the dusting until a group of women came in. By the time they were through with their various purchases, she realized she was hungry. She made herself some lunch, then carried it on a tray to the dining room so she would be close to the shop if anyone came in.

From her handbag she took some folded sheets of paper to study while she ate. Since it looked as though she were going to be a fixture in the Wagon Wheel for some time to come, she had decided she might as well learn all she could about gift shops. Last night, in line with that resolution, she had copied down some of the pointers in a booklet, *How to Run a Gift and Art Shop,* she had bought from the Superintendent of Documents in Washington for thirty-five cents. Heading the list were the words *unusual, unique, exclusive.* Those applied to the merchandise a gift shop should feature and she could see where it would be a good measuring stick for mail-order products too.

The next pointers were about stocking up on merchandise —to buy a little of everything you thought might sell, and not a lot of anything; to locate sources of supply for unusual and original centerpieces and other decorative table accessories; that attractive four- and six-piece luncheon sets were a good line to carry, as well as different cocktail and table napkins, place mats, and bridge favors.

But what interested her most of all was something entitled "The Gift and Art Shop's Wheel of Fortune Chart." Divided into pie-shaped wedges in a large circle were twelve different categories of goods to carry. They included woodcraft; metalcraft with items like book ends, pewter, hammered ash trays, copper and silver accessories, spun aluminum, and fancy jewelry. Then came glass of all kinds, including lamps and novelties; pictures, which took in all art mediums as well as pictorial maps and block prints; ceramics, which to her surprise included buttons and dress ornaments in addition to tableware and accessories like vases; plastics, textiles, and graphic arts—things like greeting cards, calendars, art books, gift books, and post cards. There was also a category called paper products that listed custom gift wrappings, artificial flowers, table sets and stationery, perfume, and miscellaneous products which took in candles, needlework, knitted goods, and toys. Leathercraft completed the list.

When she had asked Lottie why she didn't carry the full line, Lottie had pointed out that, with antiques her specialty, she couldn't spread herself in too many directions. But Holly had the feeling that somewhere in this chart she herself might find the idea for some really salable item, in addition to the period dolls which were now on their way from Florida.

The doorbell tinkled and Holly went into the shop. This time it was Craig.

"Hi!" he greeted her. "Where's Charley?"

"Out on a luncheon date."

"Oh? With some of the girls?"

She shook her head. "No. A customer." If Lottie wanted to tell him the details, that was up to her.

They were interrupted by the ringing of the phone. The voice on the other end was her mother's.

"Holly, there's someone here from Kansas to see you."

"From Kansas? For me?" She didn't try to hide her astonishment. "Who is it?"

"A Mrs. Wright. She's interested in handbags and saw your ad in *Hodgepodge*. She's driving through on the way to Maine and wants to make a selection. Where do you keep them?"

Holly's excitement evaporated. In her impatience over the lack of orders, she had given away many of her samples as presents to out-of-state friends and relatives. All she had on hand were the ones she had already used herself.

"Mine are in the second drawer of the big white chest in my room," she told her mother. "You could show her those and ask her if she'd like a copy of any. And do tell her I'm sorry I wasn't at home to meet her."

But as Holly hung up she couldn't help feeling pleased. Whatever the outcome, she had made an impression as far away as Kansas. It was something to have a person sufficiently interested in your handwork to go to the trouble of looking you up on a long trip. Happily she told Craig about it.

"I'd call that quite a feather in your cap," he commented.

"I never realized that customers would come to look me up in person." But, even as she spoke, it came to her that this was just another variation of her friend's experience. "I don't know when Lottie will be back," she added now.

"That's all right. I didn't want to see her about anything special. Just tell her I stopped by to say 'Hello.' "

"I will." Then, watching him head for the door, Holly couldn't resist a mischievous impulse to tease him.

"Craig."

He turned. "Yes?"

"Where are you going on your vacation this year?"

"Down the Housatonic by canoe," he answered, just as she had thought he would.

"Oh? Again?"

He grinned. "You ought to try it sometime."

"I can think of places I'd rather go."

"Such as?"

"Florida for one."

"Well, you're welcome to it." With a "Be seeing you," he was off.

Feeling rather deflated, Holly went on with the dusting where Lottie had left off. Craig hadn't even asked her why her choice was Florida. Wasn't he interested? In a way she would have liked to continue their verbal duel.

Quite a while later Lottie returned to the shop, looking unexpectedly animated and full of apologies. "I'm sorry I left you alone so long, Holly; but Andrew and I were so busy talking, the time just flew."

"Andrew? You mean Mr. Weatherby?"

"No. Andrew Forrester, Mr. Weatherby's friend. He was out in the car and went to lunch with us. Of all things, it turned out he came from my home town—I guess I never told you I come from Brookline, right outside of Boston—and we know a lot of the same people. You've no idea what fun we had." She sighed happily. "It really was wonderful."

"And did you discourage Mr. Weatherby—about the house, I mean?"

"Oh, completely. I told him I didn't have the slightest interest in selling."

"I'm glad."

Lottie began rearranging a jewelry display.

"Craig was here."

"Is he coming back?"

"No. He just stopped by to say 'Hello.'" And then it came to her how silly she had been. She could have asked Craig to go to the party with her.

CHAPTER

12

The day of the studio party turned out to be a beautiful one, clear but unusually cool for June. When Holly arrived soon after six, a roaring fire was already going in the great fireplace that took in almost one whole end of the barn. Several easels had been shoved against the opposite wall and a large number of canvases were stacked face to it. In the center of the floor was an improvised trestle table made by placing a long, extra-wide board on sawhorses. On this Holly noted most of the fixings for a buffet supper.

"Well, young lady, and how are you?" Dana Early's pleasant voice boomed out at her as he took her hand in his hearty grip.

"Glad you could come, Holly," welcomed Mrs. Early, a slight little person with merry eyes.

"Is there anything I can do?" Holly offered.

The artist waved an expansive hand. "Come meet these people."

The round of introductions completed, she made her way back to Mrs. Early. "I'd like to help," she persisted.

"Everything's all ready," her hostess assured her, then added, "Perhaps we will start carrying out some of the hot dishes and get supper going."

Returning to the barn with a huge kettle of wonderfully aromatic spaghetti sauce—this was one of her husband's specialties, Teresa Early had proudly told her—Holly spotted a new arrival and was so surprised she almost dropped the kettle. The thought that Craig Wilmot might be invited as a guest in his own right had never occurred to her.

He seemed equally surprised to see her.

"Well—Holly!" he smiled, coming forward to relieve her, then added, "Do you know any of these people?"

"Outside of the Earlys—no."

"I recognized some of the faces, but not the names." Putting down the kettle where their hostess directed, he returned to her. "Can I get you some food?"

"I'm not in a hurry."

"Neither am I."

They stood back from the laughing line that was advancing on the table, and chatted until Dana Early insisted that they, too, step up. Then as they juggled their heaped-up plates and looked about, they saw that all the available chairs and benches were taken.

"Looks like we'll have to sit on the floor," Holly sighed.

But Craig shook his head. "Do you see what I see?"

The center of the barn extended in an unbroken sweep to the peaked roof, but on both sides was a second floor. One was enclosed; but the other was open with a straight up-and-down peg ladder leading to it, and up there stood a graceful cutter sleigh.

"Now if we can just get our food up there without spilling it . . ." Craig led the way.

Soon they were comfortably settled on the springy seat,

from which they had removed the dust cover. As they ate they looked at the graduated bells that decorated the shafts.

"Do you suppose Mr. Early used this in a painting, Craig?"

"He might have."

"Hey! Why didn't we think of sitting there?" another couple called up to them.

"Exclusive!" yelled someone else from below but with good humor, and Holly and Craig joined in the laughter. Though they were away from the group, they were now more part of it than before. For the first time since she had arrived, Holly felt at ease.

"How's the mail order coming?" Craig asked.

"Slowly, but it's looking up a little. The lady from Kansas who came to the house the other day ordered two handbags and paid in advance. And I had quite a few inquiries this week. Also three orders." She didn't add that they had been for twenty-five cents apiece.

"You should feel encouraged."

She nodded. "I do. I have some new things in the works too," she added. She didn't go on to explain, but she was referring to the dolls. The parts had arrived; she had made the rag bodies, and the period costumes would come next.

Just then their host joined them. "You ought to can your sauce and sell it by mail," Holly told him.

"Suppose I did, how would I go about it?" he asked.

"Well, after you canned some test batches and made sure it would keep, you'd design a label listing all the ingredients."

"Supposing I didn't want to divulge them?" His voice was challenging.

Holly chuckled. "You'd have to, under the Pure Food and

Drug Act, if you wanted to sell by mail. That's one of the regulations, just like not using sugar substitutes. Besides," she added, "you wouldn't have to give away your proportions."

"And how would people get to know about my sauce?"

"You'd have to advertise in a magazine that has readers interested in fine food—one of the home-decorating ones, for example."

Dana Early beamed at her. "You seem to be quite an authority on mail order, Holly. If I ever decide to follow your advice, I'll come to you for some more information," and he started for the ladder.

"Oh, Mr. Early!" she called after him.

He turned. "Yes, my dear?"

"There's one more thing I forgot to tell you. Before you could advertise, you'd want to wrap up a jar of sauce and mail it to yourself."

He looked amused. "Why?"

"To see if it travels all right through the mail the way you've packed it."

"I'll remember that," he promised, then disappeared down the ladder.

Holly thought Craig might be laughing at her, but he wasn't. If anything, he looked rather impressed. "How do you come by all your information?"

"Reading magazines and books about mail order."

"I can't recall seeing any mail-order magazines on the stands."

"You wouldn't. They're all subscription. There's *Advance*,

Mail Order Business Magazine, Mail Order World, and
Progressive Mail Trade."

He was smiling now. "How do you tell them apart?"

"They're all quite different, really."

A head appeared above the floor and then several members of the party joined them. Soon there was quite a bantering, envious group about the sleigh.

"Say, you two, stop holding court up there! It's time for dancing. Everybody come down!" boomed the voice of their host.

Below on the dance floor Holly found herself in a group that did not include Craig. In the background someone was tuning up a fiddle.

"Choose partners, everybody!" called Dana Early, and Holly found herself in the arms of a slim blond boy who had been one of the late arrivals.

> "Swing your partners left and right,
> Swing on in till the middle of the night.
> Now promenade around the ring
> While the birdies crow and the roosters sing.
> Now home you go and don't be slow,
> It's partners all with a do-si-do."

In her astonishment Holly almost missed the promenade. Of all people, the caller was Craig. This was an accomplishment she had hardly expected of him. Presently, spotting her in the dancing sets, he waved and Holly waved back.

During one of the intervals, while her partner went to get some punch, she found herself seated next to a pleasant, white-haired woman. Holly introduced herself.

"I'm Vera Greene," her companion told her in turn. "I come from Washington Depot," she added, mentioning a village that lay to the northwest.

"Do you know many of the people here?"

Miss Greene nodded. "Quite a few."

"I can't even remember most of the names—I met so many."

"See those two girls sitting over by the wall?"

Holly spotted the attractive brunettes and nodded.

"They're sisters and they have their own kiln over in Bethlehem," she explained. "And the lady talking to Mr. Early," she went on, "comes from Newtown. She does enameling, and lectures all over the state. She belongs to the Connecticut Craftsmen too."

"What's that?" Holly wanted to know, and her companion went on to explain that it was a statewide club of people who created handmades in mediums like Swedish weaving, silk-screen printing, ceramics, and decorative tinware. Once a year, she added, they held a big fair at which they displayed and sold work and took special orders.

Making a mental note that she would have to see about becoming a member, Holly asked Miss Greene if she belonged.

"Goodness, no!" she laughed. "I'm not artistic. All I do is mend china—my work comes to me by mail—and type manuscripts, which I also get by mail."

At the mention of the word "mail," Holly's ears had pricked up. "I didn't realize you could do things like that through the mails."

"Oh, yes, people offer all kinds of services—things like developing pictures, photo retouching, mending stockings, repairing watches . . . even ghost writing."

"What's ghost writing?" inquired Holly, amused.

"That's where people write under someone else's name. Often a famous person who would like to do a book or article about his experiences, and doesn't have either the time or the know-how to get it down, gives all the facts to the 'ghost,' who is an experienced professional writer. Or people not in the public eye who have a story to tell and don't know how to present it hire a 'ghost' who advertises in the writers' magazines. That's where I advertise my typing services," she added. "I've done books, plays, stories, and articles. Do you type?"

"Yes, but it's designing and making things that interest me," and she proceeded to tell what she was doing.

"Now isn't that interesting!" exclaimed Miss Greene. "I have a friend in New York State who's in mail order too. She started out making Christmas angels for table centerpieces and tree ornaments, and got some orders from people in her home town after she had donated some to a church fair. But she wasn't earning much that way. Then someone suggested that she take her work to one of the clinics of the Women's Council."

"What's that?" Holly asked.

"It's a consulting service for women who want to start or expand a business, started by Governor Dewey as a service of the New York State Department of Commerce. Anyhow my friend went to one of these job clinics, and the women who attended it were so enthusiastic that they gave her a lot of orders. They also helped her decide on the best prices, gave her some ideas about packaging, and suggested she send samples to the editor of a home-decorating magazine."

The music had started up again, but Holly was completely carried away by the story. "What happened then?"

"The editor asked her to send in some glossy photographs of the angels; these were reproduced and mentioned in one of the magazine's shopping columns and, as a result, had a wonderful response. Now she has a full line of party favors, a large private-customer list, and runs small ads in the magazine that gave her her start."

Holly took a deep breath. It sounded like a fairy tale come true. Then she was conscious that a different voice was doing the calling and that Craig was standing in front of her.

"Dance?" he asked.

Holly excused herself and said how much she had enjoyed her talk. "I'll see you again," she smiled.

"Hope I didn't break up something," Craig commented as they went to join another set that was forming.

"Oh, no! But I never expected to run into someone here who was in mail order too."

The party grew merrier and merrier. Presently even the Fairchilds looked in on their way back from another engagement and then they, too, joined the dancers.

As a matter of course, Craig took her home. Holly smiled as they passed the side road where he had called her down about picking the northern holly. She had been so angry at him then. Now she snapped her fingers.

Craig looked in her direction.

"I've got it!" she cried. "A name for my mail-order business. I'm going to call it HOLLY HANDCRAFTS!"

All in all, it had been a most unexpected evening.

CHAPTER

13

Professor Roberts was going to stay in the Southwest. If the Elliots wanted to buy his place, they would have first chance. So ran the gist of the professor's latest letter. Holly was sure her parents wouldn't consider it. It was one thing staying on for a year, but putting down permanent roots in the country was quite different and she dismissed it from her thoughts.

Right now she was happy about a lot of things—including her catchy business name, Holly Handcrafts. Dana Early had even helped her design her letterhead, mailing label, and tie-on trademark which she spatter-painted in red and green with two stencils. When she had asked him what she owed him, he had waved aside the idea of pay.

"Who knows, I might want you to model for a magazine cover or ad sometime," he had told her, and she had been both excited over the prospect and pleased to think the design wasn't costing her anything.

Then there had been that very special letter from Duncan Moore when he received the photographs of the dolls. She had even included one of herself holding them, so he wouldn't get the idea she was an elderly spinster or something.

You have certainly done a beautiful job. I also consider it a very nice touch that you blockprinted the design on the doll's dresses yourself, to make it right in scale. The holly leaves and berries of the print team up very well with your label. One could almost call it a stroke of genius.

I shall be able to use several of the photographs in some future ads. I will pay you as they appear. Also under separate cover I am sending you several of my ceramics. You can show them to your friends and, if you receive any orders, I will pay you a commission. The pieces are for you to keep.

When the candle and flower holders and the book-end vases arrived, each piece exquisitely worked with replicas of marine life, she showed them to Lottie, who decided they would make a nice addition to her own stock and sent in an order through Holly.

"The Wagon Wheel is the gift shop in Woodbury where I work," she had explained in the accompanying letter. "I certainly don't want you to pay me a commission."

With her next small order he had sent her an additional doll head and parts. "The extra one is thanks for getting me more business," said the note that came with it. "What I need is more personal advocates like you."

Duncan Moore was a very nice contact. The only thing she regretted was that his studio was so far away. Now if he were only located in Bethlehem, like the two sisters she had met at the party, they might even make a joint venture of something like the dolls. However, advertising the period dolls had brought her quite a number of inquiries from doll hospitals which, besides mending dolls, also offered various kinds for sale. She hadn't realized before the letters came how many people ran doll hospitals in their homes. It was really remarkable the number of people who offered services and courses. The hobby and handicraft magazines listed instruction in things like glovemaking, zipper repair, candy or candle making, photography, preserving baby shoes, writing, drawing cartoons, and many others. Another government-published booklet called *Establishing and Operating a Mail Order Business,* which she had recently acquired for a quarter, mentioned that many mail-order people added to their income by selling their experience, setting it up in the form of instruction sheets or brief courses. Well, she thought, it will be some time before I can do that—but it's an idea!

In the latest issue of *Profitable Hobbies* she noticed that a man in Arkansas was offering square-dance calls and instructions. That reminded her of Craig. Since he had discovered her interest in folk dancing the night of the Earlys' party, he had invited her to the annual square-dance festival at Storrs, for which he was a caller. She had enjoyed watching the different groups, many of them in period costume, and had danced in some of the noncompeting sets herself. Craig had joined her for several dances while another caller spelled him. He was as good a dancer as he was a caller, and since then they had attended square dances nearer home. This past week end he had left for his annual two-week pilgrimage down the Housatonic by canoe.

She put the magazine away and had begun placing price lists in envelopes when she heard footsteps in the hall.

"Mother."

"Yes, dear."

"Dad isn't really considering buying this place, is he?"

Mrs. Elliot smiled. "He's doing more than that. He's just decided 'Yes.'"

"Oh, no!" Holly's exclamation was filled with dismay. "I think that's very inconsiderate of him, don't you?"

"Why inconsiderate?"

"Because he isn't thinking about the rest of us!"

"But, darling, that's where you're wrong! The boys love it here. I do too, and you—" She stopped. "I thought you did, Holly."

She shook her head. "Not for a permanent place. It's too far away. I don't have a car, and goodness knows when I'll even be able to save up for a secondhand one."

"Your Dad and I love this place because it is far out. And we do have nice neighbors." She took a deep breath. "It's too bad you feel the way you do, Holly, but one of these days you'll be having a home of your own and then you can choose the location you want. After all, if you had married Mark, you'd be gone already," she reminded her.

"I didn't marry Mark, though!" Holly hadn't meant to speak irritably, but she wished her mother wouldn't bring up the past. "You sound as though you wanted to get rid of me!" she couldn't help adding now.

"Holly! For goodness' sakes!" Her mother came over and playfully rumpled her hair. "You know we all want you home as long as possible, and we'd miss you a great deal if you went away."

Though the words were reassuring, the hurt persisted after

her mother had left. Also there was the matter of her parting remark.

"You could save up for a car if you'd stop playing around with mail order," she had said.

Holly had been taken aback. Here she had been going along clothed in the comfortable assurance that her parents thought she was showing wonderful stick-to-itiveness—and look at the opinion her mother held. One thing was sure though. If she had needed a fresh incentive to take stock and gather her forces, this was it. Already it was nearly August. According to the mail-order magazines, the stampede to buy for Christmas via the armchair route started in October. If she was to offer a line of Holly Handcrafts, she would have to start planning and making things right now.

In the evenings that followed, while she worked with her fingers, her dreams took wing. If she made out well with these handmades she was offering—bridge cloths with textile-painted holly leaves in each corner and tiny jingle bells tied on with red yarn, matching napkins with one decorated corner; a set of tumblers stenciled with a holly motif; holly-painted button earrings; the Duncan Moore dolls . . . it was possible that she could take a trip to Florida. If she could arrange it when the Fairchilds had to go to the citrus groves, she might be able to travel with them and pay her share of the gas and oil. Then, while they were busy or looking up their friends, she could travel around by herself, a jaunt which would naturally include a visit to Sarasota and Duncan Moore's studio. She could just picture his delighted surprise at her unexpected arrival.

"This is too good to be true," she could almost hear him

say in a voice as enthusiastic as his letters. "Now just as soon as I take a few things out of the kiln and feed the dog, we'll go out to dinner."

Ah, well, she told herself, dream on girl, dream on. But by the time Craig returned from his canoe trip, she was deep in folders and pamphlets on Florida.

"Make any fresh discoveries?" Holly teased the first time Craig dropped in at the shop, looking tanned and healthy.

"There's always something new to see," he told her with good humor. "I read some more books on the valley last winter and I looked up some of the spots mentioned—Lovers' Leap for one, which isn't too far from here."

"Sounds like a contest," she chuckled, "the kind we used to read about in mythology."

"This is a story handed down from Indian days," Craig went on. "It seems that, soon after the white settlers took up their homes near the mouth of the river, an Indian princess saved a white lad wandering half-starved in the woods and they fell in love. Before marrying her he went to see his people. When spring came and he hadn't returned, her father, the chief, insisted that she take a husband in the tribe. The day of the ceremony, dressed in her bridal finery, she hurried down to the river, got into a canoe below the falls of Metichawan, and headed toward the rapids swollen with the spring floods. It would have to be just then, so the legend goes, that the white boy appeared on the steep bank above, on his way back to the Indian encampment. Too late to save his fiancée, he leaped down to join her in the boiling waters below."

[120]

Holly looked at him. "It sounds like the Pocahontas story with embroidery."

"Don't you believe in romance?" Craig demanded.

"I—of course," she admitted, suddenly self-conscious at the intent way he was regarding her. Then, to draw his attention from herself, she quickly added. "I suppose that's the kind I'll run across in Florida—you know, the Fountain of Youth and—"

"Why Florida?" he demanded.

"I just happened to mention it because that's where I'm going on my vacation."

"How soon?" he wanted to know.

"Oh, not until winter. Why?"

"Because I wondered if you were going to be here Friday night."

"What's Friday night?"

"A square dance."

"I'll be here."

"Then it's a date?"

She nodded. "It sounds like fun."

Mid-afternoon on Friday, Holly was busy in the shop when the phone rang. She answered it.

"Miss Elliot?" inquired a strange voice, masculine gender. And then, when she had identified herself, "Holly, this is Duncan Moore."

"Duncan Moore!" She couldn't keep the excitement out of her voice. "Where are you calling from? Florida?"

"No. Ridgefield, Connecticut. How do I find the Wagon Wheel?"

She told him and he repeated the directions. "Don't go away," he added.

"Don't worry, I won't," she laughed. Hanging up, she looked at her wrist watch. That should bring him here just about five o'clock. And then she remembered, her heart turning over in her mouth, that this was Friday and it would be just about the time when Craig would be by to pick her up. She must call off her date with him. After all, Duncan had come all the way from Florida! Then she realized there was no way to reach Craig until he arrived.

But what if Duncan put in an appearance first? From happy excitement Holly's mood changed to one of nervousness. She was glad that Lottie was out. It would have been hard to hide her jitters.

The way things turned out, Craig was the earlier. "All set?" he greeted her.

"Oh, Craig, something's happened!" She hoped he would understand. "A friend of mine from out of town is on the way here and expects to spend the evening with me."

"That's no problem. We'll take her along with us."

"It isn't a her—it's a him."

"Oh. Didn't you tell him you had a date?"

"I—he's from Florida."

"Florida? Oh—Florida." His voice had a curiously flat sound. "Sorry if I've been so slow to catch on," and he headed for the door.

"But, Craig, you don't underst——"

"Enjoy yourself!"

In disbelief Holly heard the screen door slam, then the sound of his car starting up. With the exception of the very first time they had met, he had been so even-tempered that she was surprised at his flare of temper. He hadn't even given her a chance to explain that Duncan was a business acquaintance. Well, there wasn't anything she could do about it now and she certainly wasn't going to let his attitude spoil what promised to be an interesting evening.

It was almost six when Duncan arrived, looking exactly like his pictures and impeccable in a bow tie and lightweight brown crease-resistant summer suit. He was full of apologies —must have taken the wrong turn somewhere, he said.

"Where's the best place to eat?" he asked as he guided her out to a yellow convertible.

Holly mentioned the local inn but added it was rather expensive.

"All we're concerned with is the food," he smiled.

At the inn he commanded immediate attention. The hostess guided them to the best location in the dining room and left them with menus. He smiled at Holly, flashing even white teeth. "You have no idea how nice it is seeing you at last, Holly." Then he signaled a waitress who was already hovering solicitously in the background and began questioning her about the specialties of the house.

The meal was delicious and they chatted about many things, but the thought of Craig kept intruding and eating a hole into Holly's pleasure.

"Would you like to come out to my house and meet the family?" she questioned as they walked out to the entrance hall.

"How far away do you live?"

[123]

"Only about half an hour's drive that way," and she indicated a southerly direction.

"Hm." Duncan consulted a wafer-thin wrist watch. "I'd love to, Holly, only I'm late for an appointment already."

"An appointment at this hour?" she echoed, completely taken by surprise.

He grimaced. "Unfortunately this is business. But that's why I'm on this trip—to make contacts with buyers. This is with the gift buyer of one of the biggest stores in Hartford. And from there I continue up through New England."

Holly said nothing.

"I have to go back by way of New York State," he went on, "but maybe I'll meet your folks on my next trip." He snapped his fingers. "I know! The next time I come up to New York City—I fly sometimes—why don't you meet me there and we'll really do the town, to make up for this hasty visit?"

Holly didn't feel like committing herself. After all, she had antagonized Craig by giving up their date and now, at eight o'clock in the evening, she was about to be on her own again. But Duncan was quick to sense her mingled chagrin and reluctance.

"Holly, you must understand that I wouldn't hurry off like this if I didn't have to. It's been so wonderful to see you in person, and I would like to stay on longer. But we'll make up for lost time very soon."

With that promise he left, after calling the local taxi to take her home. On the drive back to Goodhill Road, Holly's spirits rose. After all, hadn't she taken too much for granted? He hadn't said anything about dinner and the evening. He had said he wanted to see her. They had had a little over two hours together, and he did say he would see her again. He was even more charming than she had imagined, and the very briefness of his visit had been tantalizing. Then she sighed. She had been so upset over the way Craig had acted that she had even forgotten to tell Duncan Moore that she was planning a trip to Florida.

CHAPTER

14

"It just doesn't seem right—a young person putting in as many hours as you do," her father remarked one night on his way to bed as he looked in to see what she was doing. "Aren't you going to stop soon?"

Holly nodded, conscious of the heavy late-fall rain that was lashing the windows; the gusts of wind that shook the house. It seemed that was what she was doing more and more—stopping when she was tired, rather than finishing. She was never completely caught up with the inquiries and orders any more. Before she could take care of one batch, another arrived. But this was what she had been hoping for all last year, and it had come about because she was advertising in more magazines and had also increased the size of her ads since Lottie had given her a raise. With the addition of a decorating service, the Wagon Wheel business was picking up. Mrs. Blaine was out of the shop for hours at a stretch—which meant that Holly had more responsibility as well as the entire clerical end of Lottie's mail order. Then at home she had her own paper work, and all kinds of things to make; for now she was offering more variety than ever, including some accessory and doll patterns because she realized that many of the readers of the hobby and handwork magazines in which she advertised seemed to major in making things themselves.

"Anyhow, Dad," she observed as he stood watching her trace the pattern of a rag-doll body, "I'll be playing full time once I get to Florida—and January isn't too far off."

"I'm glad you're going," he commented, then left with a "Good night."

By now she was getting back her advertising expenses plus enough extra to supply her with some of the materials she needed, and so she was able to put part of her salary from the Wagon Wheel work into her travel fund. In two months she expected to have enough. It was already arranged that she was to go with the Fairchilds, and her father approved. Her mother too, as far as that part of the projected trip went. But the last time she had brought up the subject of her southern vacation, her mother had asked if she was planning to see Duncan Moore.

"Of course I'll want to see Sarasota. And why shouldn't I visit his studio while I'm there?" she had challenged.

Her mother had given her an odd look. "Do you think it's wise to run after someone?"

Holly had taken a deep breath. "Mother, I'm not running after Duncan. After all, he is a business contact and it isn't as though he hadn't looked me up first."

"But he didn't come here to meet us. A young man always wants to meet a girl's family if he's really interested."

"Mother, who said he's romantic over me? Besides, didn't I tell you Duncan said he'd come the next time?" Holly knew she sounded annoyed, but she didn't care.

"That could be an excuse."

"You talk as though you didn't like Duncan!"

"I don't even know him, Holly."

"Then how can you criticize him?"

"After all, dear, there are certain things that are fairly obvious."

"Such as what?" she challenged, but her mother refused to elaborate. "No matter what I say, you'll see him anyhow. So what's the use of wasting my breath?"

"You act as though you didn't want me to go to Florida."

"If Florida were only the reason for your going!"

"Mother, you're imagining things."

"Am I? Then if you aren't serious about Duncan Moore, why don't you go out with Craig?"

"I'm too busy."

"Holly! That's nonsense! You can always make time to go out with someone you really like."

To that Holly made no comment. She wasn't going to tell her mother that Craig had gone out of his way to avoid her ever since she broke their date because of Duncan's visit. He rarely came to the shop now—at least not during the hours when she was around. If he did call Lottie on the phone and Holly answered, he was very formal; but there was no use explaining to Mother. Yet why was she trying to spoil the pleasure of the trip? She had never acted this way before.

Holly sighed and started getting ready for bed. This meant removing from the bedspread the many letters, completed and half-finished orders, string, wrapping paper, and other things which had accumulated in the course of the evening. Among these was the latest issue of the *Goodhill Gazette*, which had come out that day.

MARK LOGAN CLAIMS HOMESTEAD
ON KENAI PENINSULA

the headline proclaimed. Holly knew why Mark kept writing the Fairchilds—he wanted her to know what he was doing and to feel bad because she hadn't gone with him. Well, she didn't. Just imagine if she had ended up marrying Mark! She might never have contacted Duncan through his ad and come to know him. In spite of what her mother had said, she knew Duncan had a special interest in her. She could tell from the way he wrote, his stop to see her, the date in New York he was planning. What if things went slowly between them? It was better than rushing things the way she and Mark had, only to discover they didn't think and feel alike. Holly flipped off her bedside light and, almost at once, dropped off to sleep.

The next morning Lottie herself brought up the subject of Duncan. "Holly, I don't know if you realize it; but the twenty-eighth of October I sent an order to Duncan Moore for repeats on some of the best-selling ceramics. I haven't received a confirmation or a shipment."

"That isn't a bit like him. But then I suppose he has so many orders he's all jammed up. Want me to drop him a line?"

"Please. Those candle and flower sets especially make a very good item."

The days that followed were even busier, with the accelerated tempo of Christmas shopping both at the store and by mail. Sometimes she felt that if it hadn't been for the matter of showing her mother and Mark she could realize her dreams, she would gladly have thrown the idea of mail order overboard and just concentrated on her daytime job. Also, and this was a great disappointment, the Duncan Moore dolls just didn't seem to be selling. She even had several on display at the Wagon Wheel and, while people oh'd and ah'd over them, they remained on the shelf. The fact that she was actually getting reorders on some of her new mail-order offerings, such as the holly-shaped pot holders and the quilted coffee cozies with appliquéd holly leaves and berries, didn't make up for it either.

Another thing that bothered her was Lottie's exasperation at Duncan. In response to the letter Lottie had asked her to write, Duncan replied that he had discontinued making that particular line; but if the Wagon Wheel wanted to carry ceramic flamingos, he was now making those.

"I don't need flamingos in the shop any more than a cat needs two tails!" Lottie had exploded in one of her rare angry moments. "Couldn't he have written me earlier—as soon as he received my order—to say he was discontinuing the shell-decorated pieces?"

"I guess he was too busy," Holly interposed.

"Too busy!" sputtered Lottie. "Then he should get himself a secretary. You can't carry on a business in a haphazard fashion. Rule number one is to answer your mail when it comes in. I have special orders for some of those pieces. Because of Duncan Moore's vagaries, I may be losing good customers."

For the first time since she had known Lottie, Holly was put out with her. But all she said was, "I guess when you're an artist, you get tired of doing the same thing."

"Then he should concentrate on designing new pieces and let someone else make them up!"

Holly didn't see any point in prolonging the argument. There was nothing she could say to change Lottie's mind about Duncan. Apparently he was doing a good business, and she didn't suppose he would even feel the loss of orders from the Wagon Wheel.

One evening when she was snowed under with an even larger than usual mail, and in an effort to ease the continued tension between her mother and herself, Holly jokingly asked if she wouldn't like to go into partnership with her. "I know you don't like to make things with your hands," she added, "but perhaps you'd enjoy the paper work."

"Thanks just the same, but I'll soon be having plenty of paper work of my own."

Holly looked her surprise.

"I'm going back to teaching the second semester—over in Washington. I know it means getting another car," she continued, "but I've had a long rest and change and I'm looking forward to getting back to a classroom."

This was something Holly hadn't expected. And perhaps, once she was occupied with running classes as well as the house, her mother would stop being in a state of mind over Duncan and her. At least she hoped so.

A few weeks before Christmas and at the very height of her busyness, Holly took time out to do something just for fun. Gathering Christmas greens in the woods with Hugh and Roy, she cut some twigs shaped like miniature trees. Back at home she mixed up a bowlful of plaster of Paris; spooned it into small scrubbed flowerpots plugged with modeling clay; and, as the mixture thickened, inserted a twig in each pot. Later, using a flit gun, she sprayed the tiny trees and pots with gold metallic paint.

"Holly, they're beautiful!" exclaimed her mother with unexpected enthusiasm.

"Just wait till they're decorated—you'll like them even better," she promised, and started tying on tiny, varicolored Christmas balls.

Later, against the greens on the mantle, the golden trees looked like fabulous Christmas-display props borrowed from an elegantly expensive Fifth Avenue show window. Even the boys chorused their approval.

In odd moments within the next week she made up and decorated half a dozen more; then one evening when the stores were open and the family had shopping to do in Waterbury, she took along the miniature holiday trees.

"Of course you never can tell about things like these," the gift-shop owner to whom she showed them told her, "but if they do go, they ought to bring at least three dollars apiece. Why don't you leave them here and see what happens?"

Holly agreed. Lottie would have taken them on consignment too, but she hadn't wanted to impose on her friendship. Also acceptance by a stranger had made it more of a test.

Back home she made up some more to give as gifts. She also made some assorted Christmas candies without which the family had never considered Christmas complete. She sent one box to Duncan by first-class air mail. Another she gave to Lottie with a golden tree, saying it was just a little something for her sweet tooth.

The Sunday after New Year's and two weeks before Holly

would be leaving for Florida, Lottie dropped by. "I was afraid I'd find you indoors," she told Holly, who was writing out some new ads. "Did you know the skiing is wonderful at the Fairchilds'?"

Holly shook her head. "No, I didn't."

"Have you got some skis?"

"No."

"Well, I had an extra pair at the house and I brought them along just in case. Get dressed and we'll be on our way."

"I don't know much about skiing," Holly protested. "Hugh and Roy had some skis one winter and we all took turns, but that was a long time ago."

"Oh, come on! You need some good fresh air and exercise. You don't want to turn into a hothouse plant, do you?"

And so Holly let herself be persuaded. When she and Lottie arrived, the Fairchilds and some of their friends were already using the slope north of the house.

"Do you jump?" Clem Fairchild asked her, and, when Holly said she didn't, he cautioned her to head for the west side of the lake, which would take her across the wide earth dam. At all costs she must avoid the south end, where the rock-retained embankment fell steeply away to the snow-covered ice.

"I'll probably start two feet from the bottom of the hill," she joked. But after a few tries on one of the gentler slopes, she gained confidence and went up to a steeper one. It was frightening and yet exhilarating. She was very glad that Lottie had persuaded her to come, until on one of their treks up the hill she saw Craig standing at the top of the slope.

"Hi," he greeted her and Lottie.

Holly tried to say "Hello" without looking self-conscious.

"Found your note at the shop," he told his cousin. "Where did you say my skis were?" Then his eyes fell on the ones Holly had on.

"Oh, are these yours?" She knelt down to remove them. "I should be getting home anyhow."

"Go ahead, use them."

"I'm not going to keep you from your skis."

"Holly, take mine," Lottie cut in. "I've had enough for a while and I'm going into the house to get warm."

"But I don't want to spoil your fun," Holly protested.

"You will if you interfere with my rest cure," Lottie replied.

After that there was nothing to do but accept. However, Craig's appearance had spoiled her day. She would go down a few times more, then call it an afternoon.

She was about to take off when Craig's voice recalled her. "This time try flexing your knees a little more."

"How much do you charge an hour for instructions?" she asked, telling herself she had done all right till now.

He took no notice of her sarcasm. "With a little more practice, you could be pretty good."

Pretty good! She'd show him. Craig Wilmot didn't have to act so patronizingly. Up to now she hadn't had the courage to try the very steepest slope, but now her dander was up and she headed for it. Once he saw her glide downhill with effortless grace and swoop across the wide earthen dam, he would feel very foolish about having tried to tell her what to do. But as soon as she took off, panic gripped her. The slope was at more of an angle than she had realized. The skis were picking up speed. She tried to stop but couldn't. She was going faster and faster. She was conscious of someone yelling her name. In nightmarish fright she sensed that the skis were leaving the ground. Almost in the next moment the snowy surface of the lake was coming up to meet her with incredible swiftness, and then she felt a terrible numbness in one of her legs.

CHAPTER

15

HOLLY ELLIOT BREAKS ANKLE
IN SKIING ACCIDENT
TO BE IN CAST TWELVE WEEKS

Reading the feature story in the *Goodhill Gazette*, Holly sighed. Home after three days in the hospital, she had a plaster cast that extended from the toes of her right foot to her hip and a pair of crutches with which she couldn't even navigate the stairs, so that she had to sleep on the couch in her father's study. It would be impossible for her to go on with her job at the Wagon Wheel. Worse still, the trip to Florida was off. Unfortunately her mishap was affecting her family too. Just at a time when her father was having the added expense of paying off on the house, she had had to run up a big hospital and doctor bill. And then, because of the care she would need, her mother wouldn't accept the teaching job.

If only Dad had said, "Look at all the money your accident is costing, when I already have heavy obligations"! Or if her mother had added, "Just because you wanted to show off, I'm stuck at home and can't go back to my teaching." But her parents acted serenely cheerful.

"You know, darling, you could just as easily have broken your neck," her father had remarked in his usual mild manner while she was in the hospital. "Your mother and I feel very grateful that you're alive and that you won't have any permanent injuries from your fall. The surgeon didn't have to put a silver bolt in your ankle after all."

Hugh and Roy had stared at her with awed eyes when her father, with Craig's help, brought her home from the hospital. Craig assisted the local doctor in putting temporary splints around her ankle after she had been given a hypo the afternoon of the accident. He and Lottie had sent her a huge bouquet of yellow roses while she was at the hospital. In his place she wouldn't have been so solicitous.

"I don't see why you're being so nice to me," she told him when he came to call three days in succession.

"It's nothing," he deprecated. "Anyhow," he added with one of his slow, rare smiles, "I expect you'd come to see me, too, if I were laid up."

"Of course," she agreed, "only I hope you'll never break an ankle. Or Lottie either," she added.

"Speaking of Lottie, she feels very bad about having persuaded you to go skiing."

Holly was distressed over this piece of news. "Oh, but please tell her I don't blame her in the least. I could have said 'No.' And taking the steep slope was my own idea. I'd like to see her when she has the time. I know she's terribly busy. And then she'll have all the trouble of breaking in new help—"

"Don't worry about Lottie."

"I'll try not to."

He rose. "Well, see you soon."

Holly nodded. "And thanks for coming." Even if his visits were in the line of duty, they were welcome. But the person she most wanted to see—Duncan—was completely out of reach. How, she wondered, would he react when he heard the news? Right now she didn't have the heart to write him.

To add to her discouragement, one of her handbag patterns—a drawstring style decorated scatter-fashion with lots of tiny bells and bows—which she had sent to one of the big pattern companies, hoping that they would buy it, had been returned with a "Thank you for letting us see it, but at present we are overstocked."

The Fairchilds came to say good-bye the night before leaving for Florida, and after they left Holly felt worse than ever. But for her accident, she might now be headed down the coast with them on her way to surprising Duncan.

Several days later, just about the time the Fairchilds should be reaching Florida, her mother came in to say that there was a long-distance call for her and did she want to take it herself.

Holly reached for her crutches, then stumped slowly out through the living room and into the hall. If Alice and Clem were nice enough to phone to see how she was, the least she could do was answer.

But the voice on the other end was Duncan's.

"Hi, Holly, how are you? I just got in from Florida."

Excitement gripped her. "Are you near here?"

"New York."

"Oh."

"What's the matter?" he chuckled. "Don't sound so dis-

appointed. I want you to come down. We'll have ourselves
a big time."

"But, Duncan, I can't. I broke my ankle."

"You what?" He sounded incredulous.

Holly repeated the information and told him how it had
happened.

Duncan was all solicitude. "My dear, I'm sorry as I can
be to hear about your accident. I'd like to get up to see you,
but I'm going to be tied up with all sorts of business appoint-
ments."

"Oh." Did her voice, she wondered, sound as deflated as
she felt?

"Meanwhile take care of yourself and let me know how
you get along."

"I will," she agreed, knowing full well she wouldn't. She
told herself things would have been different if she hadn't
been cast-ridden. She would have gone to New York and—
Then she remembered. She would have been almost to Sarasota now and she wouldn't have found Duncan there. The
trip to Florida would have turned out to be a fool's errand.
Slowly she made her way back to the study.

"That was Duncan," she told her mother in an attempt
to pass it off lightly. "He's in New York. He wanted me to
do the town with him. Wouldn't I have made the perfect
playmate?" she laughed.

Her mother rose to her mood. "Oh, I don't know. I can
imagine worse."

Back in her father's easy chair, Holly stared off into space.
So her mother had been right. She had built up a romantic
relationship that had never existed. How could she have been

so stupid? Well, she told herself, Holly Elliot, you stop feeling sorry for yourself. Do something to make the time count instead of just sitting around. Unexpectedly a line of poetry from highschool English came back to her—"Be the pilot of your fate, the captain of your soul," she paraphrased. These past weeks she had wallowed in a sea of self-pity. Thinking of some of the people completely bedridden who carried on a mail-order business under worse conditions made her ashamed. The months ahead should be good for something. While she hadn't realized it, now was the time to take stock of the Holly Handcrafts situation. Even if she couldn't run a sewing machine, she did have the use of her hands. She could type envelopes and answer inquiries. In fact, she could do all kinds of handwork, read more books on mail order, and catch up on back numbers of her hobby magazines.

When her mother came in to bring her a glass of orange juice and to see if there was anything she wanted, Holly said the next time she had to go upstairs would she bring the pile of magazines on her bedside table. Over her protests she went right away and soon Holly was busy going through the magazines.

Presently a line was jumping out at her. *A recipe for success in establishing a mail-order business is to start out with one item and plug it for all you're worth.*

That was something she hadn't done. In her anxiety for quick results and big returns, she had spread herself all over the lot. She should have concentrated on one offering, like the Duncan Moore period doll. If only she could get it to move, she would continue to order the ceramic parts from

Duncan even though their relations would be strictly business from now on.

A surprise visitor turned up that evening. She hadn't seen Miss Greene since the studio party at the Earlys' last May.

"I read about your accident in the *Newtown Bee*," she told Holly. "I've had you on my mind even though I haven't been over till now. In fact, I wrote my friend who has the mail-order business about you." Now she handed her a large mailing envelope. "She had the New York Women's Council and the New York State Chamber of Commerce send these on to me for you. I would have mailed it, only I kept thinking I'd see you; and when I read what had happened, I didn't want to delay my visit any longer."

Holly couldn't refrain from opening it at once. There were all kinds of pamphlets, including *102 Ideas for a Business of Her Own* and *Selling by Mail,* and then some mimeographed case histories covering some of the career clinics, which she had completely forgotten.

"Another thing you may not know," Miss Greene added, "is that you can get advice on packaging and a lot of other things from one of the regional departments of commerce, either by mail or in person. There happens to be one in Hartford."

After a little more talk her visitor left, saying she didn't want to tire her. However, Holly was anything but tired. Even after her mother helped her get comfortable for the night, she continued to go through the pamphlets and actual experience stories. And two things stood out clearly. One was that the best price for mail-order items was between one and five dollars. The other was that one path to free publicity and advertising lay in sending a sample of your advertised product to woman's-page editors, radio and television commentators, and magazine shopping-column editors. But the Duncan Moore doll, even if she did put the price down to five dollars, was hardly the type of item one could blithely hand out as a free sample. At least she could try the lower price and see if three dollars less made a difference in customer response.

The next day she continued her study of the materials. Something she hadn't been conscious of before was the importance of packaging and what a silent salesman it was for your offerings. Actually there was a bewildering amount of information to master on this subject alone—many facts which she had overlooked before, such as the startling news that boxes for commercial products could not be too much out of line in either size or shape with what was inside or one would be violating the mail-order statutes and be open to prosecution.

Later Holly leafed through a new grocery-store magazine her mother had left with her. One section was devoted to all kinds of patterns for things to make. Why hadn't she thought of this magazine or one of its competitors for a design market? It might be worth a try, sending them the rejected handbag idea. Better still, why not send it in with a matching headband—say a wide velvet or grosgrain ribbon, or any desirable piece of fabric folded double and stitched together. Then a halo clip headband could be inserted and the ends turned under, and the side that showed could be scatter-trimmed with bows and bells.

After dinner, although there had been a heavy snowfall during the night, Craig and Lottie stopped to see her.

"You're looking a lot better than the first time I was here," Lottie remarked, and Craig agreed.

Holly gave a little laugh. "I think I'll live. At least I'm keeping myself busy." She scrutinized Lottie. "You're looking wonderful. Have you found someone to help you yet?"

Lottie shook her head. "Guess I'll live too," she remarked—a trifle self-consciously, Holly thought. As if by a prearranged signal, Craig excused himself and went into the living room with her parents.

"I couldn't wait to show you this," Lottie told her. "That's why I persuaded Craig to bring me out this wintry evening." She held out her left hand. On the third finger was an engagement ring.

"Lottie! How wonderful! Who is he?"

Lottie smiled. "Remember my mentioning Andrew?"

"Andrew—I—" Holly puzzled over this. "The only Andrew you ever spoke to me about was the one you met the day you went out with that funny little Mr. Weatherby."

"He's the one."

"You never said a word about it," Holly reproached her. Then she held out her hand. "I'm ever so happy for you, Lottie."

"Thanks. I'm pretty happy myself. After a perfect marriage that had to end because of a drunken driver—"

This was the only reference Lottie had ever made to her first marriage, and Holly marveled again at how cheerful she had always been—at least outwardly. And all the time she had ascribed her friend's good spirits to her being rid of a husband with whom she hadn't been happy!

[143]

"Think I'll tell your mother and Dad," said Lottie as Craig appeared in the doorway.

"Like to play some Shanghai rummy?" he asked.

Holly nodded. It was as good a way as any of passing the evening.

CHAPTER

16

The March issue of *Hodgepodge* carried a little notice about her mishap. A few days later the deluge started. Women and girls from many parts of the country, all of them strangers, sent her get-well cards and little notes of sympathy. Some of them even enclosed small gifts—a hand-stenciled handkerchief, a novel sachet, a straw lapel pin in the shape of a little burro. And, because the editors had mentioned that she collected dolls, several of the doll makers sent her examples of their work— an Ozark hillbilly, a cowboy, a Cherokee Indian, a little old lady called Aunt Het, and a hula dancer.

All in all, it was very heart-warming to find she had so many friends by mail. It had been quite unexpected and wonderful. For days the letters and surprises continued.

Holly had learned through the magazine that when a collector received a gift he sent one in return. Little by little she managed to put something of her own in the mail—earrings, and one of her small rag dolls for the doll people. Besides, she made up different things to send to the magazine to give as gifts. This would mean mention without having to pay for an additional ad.

One day the needlework editor of the grocery-store magazine wrote that they were interested in her Beaux and Belles design, the halo-clip hat and handbag, and wondered if she could send actual samples of the set. Holly followed through at once, but now she faced another period of waiting. What made it worse was the fact that she was very low in cash, with no salary, too many seasonal handmades on her mail-order list, and continuing ads to keep her name before the public. Even the travel fund had dwindled to five dollars, because she had used it to purchase necessary materials.

She had been completely housebound except for one trip to the hospital when her original cast had been taken off and replaced by a below-the-knee affair termed a walking cast. But it was still very cumbersome and required the use of crutches. She still found that moving about was trying, and she was grateful that she had her mail-order and design projects to keep her occupied.

Since the days had grown milder, her mother had taken to spending more and more time working in the yard every day. On occasion she pressed the boys into helping, but more often she raked and spaded the new beds by herself.

"I'm going to have a rock garden," she told Holly, "and a patch of really early lettuce. I never knew until I read up on it that you could pop in lettuce and radish seeds as early as the ground can be worked. And wait till you see the flowers and other vegetables we're going to have! Now that we're permanently settled, I'm going to put in a lot of perennials too!"

One afternoon while her mother was happily engaged in her favorite occupation, and Holly was sitting in front of an open window watching, a florist's delivery truck drove up and a gangling man got out.

"Is this the house of the Hollies?" she heard him ask.

"My daughter, Holly Elliot, lives here, if that's what you mean."

Drawing a slip out of his pocket, he consulted it; then broke into a low chuckle that ended on a high note. "Oh, yep, that's it. Guess I got confused. Well, I got something pretty big here."

The something pretty big turned out to be a gardenia bush larger than any Holly had ever seen. "Forty-five blossoms—count 'em," the deliveryman announced. "My boss told me to tell you to be sure you took notice of how many, because that's the number the gent wanted—he was very particular on that point when he talked to him over the phone—and that's why it took so long to fill the order."

Even without looking at the card, Holly knew it was from Duncan. He must have ordered it when he was in New York well over a month ago, since it came from a New York florist. No wonder he hadn't written since then, expecting acknowledgment of the gardenias! They were filling the room with their exotic fragrance and beauty. But why couldn't he have settled for a small sheaf of cut flowers or a colorful potted plant delivered when her mood was at low ebb? Perfectionist that he was, it had to be forty-five gardenias—no more, no less. A lavish gesture. Even her mother was surprised.

But as she penned her thank-you note, she couldn't help wishing that this could have happened earlier. Without meaning to, Duncan had failed her when she had needed him most. Craig was the one who had gone out of his way to divert her. Not that she could ever feel romantic about him! But he was good company and had a nice sense of humor, even though they disagreed about so many things. He was so carefully deliberate in his attitude toward his work and people! Unlike her, he rarely took a chance. She could hardly call him a dull person. He did have a sense of fun; he did love to dance, but he certainly had a temper.

The advent of the growing gardenias, however, was the start of an upswing. First she received a letter with a twelve-dollar check from the gift shop in Waterbury where she had left the golden trees. "We've been waiting for you to come in," she read. "All but one of the decorated trees sold and that didn't move because it was topheavy. Actually we could have sold quite a few more if we had had them. Do plan on at least several dozen as a starter for this coming Christmas season. We would like a first delivery early in November."

This in itself was enough to make her feel a little better. But then came even more exciting news. The grocery-store magazine had decided to feature her halo-clip hat and matching drawstring bag. Would seventy-five dollars for the idea be satisfactory? Also they would like her to make up four more sets untrimmed—they specified the fabrics and colors they wished. Mentally Holly calculated the cost. At most, the hats and handbags wouldn't set her back more than a dollar apiece. As for the price she would be getting for the design, it was like found money. Just imagine how long it would take her to earn the same amount making and selling earrings!

"It's no more than I expected of you," Craig commented when she told him about it. "You can do anything you set your mind to." Then his glance took in the gardenia plant.

"Don't you think it's pretty?" she inquired, mischief in her eyes.

Craig ignored her question. "I'd rather see a pot of Connecticut holly any day. That's something that would last."

"What makes you think gardenias don't last?" she challenged.

"The holly is a hardier plant. Gardenias turn yellow at the drop of a hat."

"I don't believe it!" Holly said just as Lottie came out of the kitchen, where she had been helping with refreshments.

"Hey, you two, stop bickering!" she ordered.

But Craig refused to be silenced. "Charley, stop trying to throw your weight around. No one tells me to shush!"

"Don't you think Holly deserves special treatment tonight?"

"Why tonight more than any other night?" he demanded.

"After all, it isn't every day a girl has some designs accepted."

"Congratulations," he commented, getting up. "Well, think I'll see if I can make myself useful in the kitchen."

"Don't pay any attention to Grumpy," said Lottie when her cousin was out of earshot. "I guess he's just allergic to gardenias—when someone else sends them," she winked.

So Craig was jealous. But Holly didn't have time to think about it, for Lottie changed the subject.

"If I were you," she was saying, "I'd concentrate more on dreaming up ideas, and have other people do the routine work of making them up from patterns and samples—that is, for mail order," she added. "That way you'd also have more time to get up designs for magazines and pattern companies.

Holly agreed it would be nice. All too well did she remember the hectic time of the pre-Christmas season last year. But where would she find help?

"I'm sure there must be farm women and others around in this part of the country who would like spare-time money. Then you could advertise in a magazine like *Hodgepodge* for assistance by mail. While your profit on each item wouldn't be as much, you would have more to sell—so you'd be better off."

"It sounds good," Holly agreed. "But if I take your advice, I'll certainly be busy making up samples and directions!"

"A good thing you have a Christmas business," Lottie told her. "Since it's only March, you'll have plenty of time to plan and work ahead for September or October advertising."

It was true that, with her holly trademark and holly-decorated wares, her accent, at least for the moment, should be seasonal.

"Perhaps by the time you have everything set, you'll be able to come back to the shop again. If Andy and I decide to get married after Christmas, I'd feel so much better if you were in charge while we were on our honeymoon."

"I'd love to, Lottie, if I can manage it with my own mail order."

Just then Craig and her mother came in, both carrying trays.

"Well, we won't worry about that now. It's only March," Lottie told her.

But, in the days that followed, Holly worried about something else—how to finance the Christmas catalogue she hoped to have. Actually it would be a folder with photographs and descriptions of her offerings, but she wanted it printed and she knew this was likely to run into quite a bit of money. Also, if she carried out Lottie's suggestion, she would need materials with which to supply the people who worked for her, as well as for her samples, patterns, and payment for the finished work. Was it, she wondered, a bigger operation than she could go into this year?

Then she recalled a statement from the government mail-order bulletin that people starting out in mail-order often sold their know-how to help finance their mail-order business in the getting-started years. If she had known a year and a half ago all she did now, she might not have gone through so much trial and error. With Hugh's help she could get out a number of mimeographed sheets to be called "Mail Order Tips," and offer them for a dollar in the classified columns of some of the magazines in which she advertised. Perhaps that would give her the money for the catalogue and—

"Holly, Western Union has a telegram for you. Do you want to come to the phone yourself?"

"Yes, Mother."

By now she was expert on crutches and moved quickly. She could even get up and down the stairs with one crutch and was sleeping in her own room again.

"The message," the Western Union operator informed her after she had identified herself, "is from Sarasota, Florida. It says, " 'Congratulations on your wonderful achievement in selling hat design. This I feel sure is the start of bigger and better things. All my best. Duncan.' "

"Please send a copy out to me," Holly requested. This reply to her latest letter was something to put with her keepsakes. While Craig took what she did as a matter of course, Duncan knew what it meant to have an acceptance in a highly competitive field.

Thinking of Duncan again put her in mind of the ceramic period doll. Shouldn't she risk at least one and send it to the shopping editor of a big magazine to see what reaction there would be?

But several days later, with the doll on its way, her copy for "Mail Order Tips" both written and stenciled, ready for mimeographing, and several classified ads announcing it en route to magazines, Holly began to feel restless. Such a wonderful balmy day and here she was housebound! Disconsolately she moved over to the window as Craig drove into the yard.

"How'd you like to come along while I do some checking up in this section?" he called to her.

After the way he had acted the other night she felt a little self-conscious, and Craig, sensing her hesitation, added, "It will do you good to get out."

"If you really want to know"—and now she smiled—"you must be a mind reader. I'm dying for a change."

For a while she gave herself up to the sheer delight of riding around the countryside again. Then she began to think about a remark Craig had made sometime ago, and that led to talk about conservation—his favorite subject.

"Why is so much fuss made about conservation?" Holly asked.

"Because without conservation practices much of the land might turn to unproductive wasteland, and various forms of plant and animal life would become extinct. Each state has its own special lists. In Connecticut, for example, the state flower, the mountain laurel, is protected. Also there's the dogwood, ground pine, bittersweet, and Connecticut holly."

"You don't have to tell me about the last one," she admitted ruefully, then added, "But the other night you said something about northern holly in pots. Would that be possible?"

Scrutinizing both sides of the road, he drove along until he came abreast of a clump of the still-leafless shrubs. "If you'll notice," he told her, "there are smaller shoots around the base of the parent plants. Those have grown from seeds."

Already Holly could see an illustration in her catalogue, a small, green-painted tub with a holly plant and a block of copy reading: FOR THE FIRST TIME ANYWHERE . . . A LIMITED QUANTITY OF LIVE CONNECTICUT HOLLY. Then she snapped her fingers and Craig turned to look at her.

"I have it!" she cried. "A wonderful new name for my mail-order business. I never really liked the sound of Holly Handcrafts." Recalling the deliveryman with his mix-up about her name had made it jell. From now on it would be known as HOUSE OF HOLLY.

CHAPTER

17

"The Duncan Moore doll is indeed intriguing. If you could furnish us with a glossy print showing the doll off to advantage, and with descriptive copy, we will be glad to run it—without obligation on your part —in the October issue."

That had been in April. Now, in mid-October, Holly was incredulous over the number of orders that had come in since the first of the month. Already she had enlisted the help of different women in the farm bureau and various people she had contacted by mail. She had even phoned Miss Greene to ask if she knew any people handy with the needle who would like some extra work. Also she had wired Duncan for two hundred more sets of doll parts to supplement the fifty she already had, and asked him to stand by for further orders.

She was becoming more and more involved with dolls. During the summer, soon after she had discarded her cane, she had designed a doll with a body that was three graduating circles—no arms or legs—and called it "Cuddle Cutie, the Circle Doll." The grocery-store magazine that had taken the hat and handbag bought it.

However, everything hadn't gone according to schedule. The beautiful Connecticut holly that was to have been one of her feature items, and which her mother and Craig had started for her from frost-cured seeds in pots sunk to their rims in the garden, wouldn't be big enough to sell this year. Also she hadn't made enough money on any of her enterprises to afford a mailing folder.

Considering the way things were working out now with the Duncan Moore doll, she was actually relieved that she wasn't having her mailing piece for the Christmas trade this year. She was kept busy making up extra sample dolls for her helpers to use as a model. She was hand-blockprinting with the tiny holly design yards and yards of muslin, which she bleached herself, to be used for all the doll dresses. Answering the regular mail, tracing her patterns for making doll bodies when the supply ran short, and typing out mailing labels for finished orders also took a lot of time. Hugh, for a consideration, had taken over her bookkeeping. A great deal of trial and error, hard work, and study had preceded what she termed this "lucky break" with the dolls—which in turn would help make a many-sided HOUSE OF HOLLY a reality, and also help her repay her father for at least some of her hospital and doctor bills.

To her surprise her mother had taken over the packing of the finished dolls. Her interest in flower-growing had kept her from looking for a teaching contract this fall. Already she was turning her hobby into profit by selling some of her plants to a florist, and to motorists who saw her sign for potted plants. These included those started from orange, lemon, and grapefruit seeds; coleus, a plant with brilliantly marked leaves which she raised from slips; different kinds of ivy; begonias, geraniums, and Mexican shrimp plants.

"Why don't you sell some of them by mail?" Holly suggested, but her mother didn't see why she should bother to spend money on advertising when she already had regular outlets.

If it hadn't been for Craig she wouldn't have taken any time off, but he kept insisting that she come to a square dance or a movie. When she protested that she couldn't spare the time, he always said she could work better for the change.

"Who do you think you are, my doctor?" she teased.

"You can do worse than listening to ole Doc Wilmot."

"Old?" she hooted.

"Well, I'm just a little bit older and a little bit wiser in the ways of the world than you."

"Sez who?" she laughed.

"Sez me."

"For an old-timer, Doc, you sure step lively on the dance floor."

"Must be my dancing keeps me young," he quipped.

But, along with their good times, there were occasions when Craig made her angry.

"Don't you think you're spreading yourself too much on this doll deal?" he asked one night on the way home.

"What makes you say that?"

"For an operation like this—the rate at which your orders are coming in—you really need a factory."

"I couldn't afford to rent even a small one."

"But doesn't it bother you getting into something this big without the right setup?"

"No," she blithely assured him, "it doesn't worry me at all."

"And when you're dependent on just one supplier—" he persisted.

"There's nothing wrong with my supplier." Nothing except that he doesn't call and he doesn't write, she added to herself. Nevertheless Duncan must still be interested in her, for at Easter he had sent her the most beautiful orchid corsage air mail from Florida—a tropical spraylike variety—with an accompanying note saying, "Don't forget we have a date to go dancing. As ever, Duncan." He had even sent her mother a huge pot of hyacinths—pink and white and blue. But this was October, and romance via the R.F.D. left much to be desired. Time had passed—over nine months—since her accident and still she hadn't been out of the Housatonic Valley.

One morning toward the end of October, Lottie called her up.

"I hate to interrupt when you're so busy with the doll orders, Holly. I don't suppose there's even a chance of your helping me through the Christmas season."

"I wish I could, but I don't see how."

"Well, I'm glad your business is booming. But one thing I'm going to insist on, honey chile. You know the little golden tree you gave me last Christmas? I'd like a group of those for the shop—complete with decorations. You can have the boys help, can't you?"

"I'll get them out somehow," she promised.

Up to now she had had orders for four to six dolls a day,

and on one record Saturday a dozen. Suddenly the mail orders began to multiply. One day there were twenty-four letters, the next thirty. She sent a frantic wire to Duncan:

SWAMPED WITH ORDERS STOP PLEASE RUSH THE HUNDRED I ORDERED AND GET TWO HUNDRED MORE IN THE WORKS EVEN IF YOU HAVE TO HIRE HELP

When there was no answer, a period during which the orders continued to avalanche, she grew uneasy and decided to put in a person-to-person call to Sarasota. The fear in the back of her mind was one she didn't dare voice even to herself.

Duncan answered the operator.

"Didn't you get my letter and wire?" she challenged him.

"My, Holly, but it's good to hear your voice! Matter of fact, I was going to write you today."

"Is something wrong?"

"Oh, no, everything's fine. Couldn't be better."

"Then you've shipped my order and started work on the reorder?"

There was a pause at the other end of the wire. "That's what I was going to write you about. I'm not making the dolls any more."

"You what?" Holly was incredulous.

"That's right. I'm up to my neck filling orders on my new line—the hibiscus candelabra, angelfish candlesticks, and matching salts and peppers."

"But, Duncan, you've just got to help me out! I have over two hundred orders now. Besides, you said yourself you'd

[158]

like to promote the dolls in a big way. Here's your chance—
and it isn't costing you anything for advertising."

"I know, but I'm not interested in the doll any more."

"Duncan"—she was desperate now—"I've just got to fill
those orders, and I'm afraid more will be coming in too."

"I'm sorry if it's put you on the spot, Holly."

One supplier. This was what Craig had cautioned her
about, but she had been too cocky to listen. "But it doesn't
have to, Duncan, if you get some other people to make them."

"You know I don't work that way. Everything that comes
out of this studio is done by me or not at all."

"Could I buy the master molds from you?"

"I'll give them to you—do what you want with them. I'll
even ship them air mail special."

"I'd appreciate it if you would." Though her voice was
calm, she could feel herself trembling with indignation. Now
she knew how Lottie had felt last year. If she could not find
a ceramist to help her, she would really be out of luck. She
remembered the sisters from Bethlehem who ran a kiln, but
she couldn't recall their names. When she phoned the ever-
helpful Miss Greene in Washington Depot, she gave her the
information.

Eileen and Frances Sheldon were unexpectedly under-
standing. It was a busy time for them, but they promised to
do what they could.

And still the orders continued to pour in. To Holly's
relief the molds reached her sooner than she had hoped, and
the sisters got to work and also hired some skilled help. Even
her father rose to the occasion by detouring to Bethlehem,
every afternoon when he was through with his day's teach-

ing, to bring carefully cushioned cartons of doll heads, arms, and legs home to her for distribution. She was so busy with work that she was just barely conscious of anything that wasn't directly concerned with getting more dolls made. There wasn't even time to indulge herself in writing an angry letter to Duncan. Also, after he had sent her the master molds, what could she say?

For the first time since she had been in mail business, she lived in hopes that the orders would start to taper off; but they continued in an ever-increasing tide. The five-hundred mark was reached, and it went on and on until Holly was afraid to ask Hugh what the latest figure was. The finished dolls seemed to be moving so slowly off her personal assembly line that she didn't seem to be making any progress at all.

"It's like the many-headed Hydra in mythology," she told her mother. "Cut off one of the serpent's heads and two appear in its place. Only in my case it seems we get five in return for each one we send out."

By mid-November the orders had reached the incredible figure of thirteen hundred and seventy-four. Of these only one hundred and seventy-six had been filled. She alone knew what a tremendous effort they represented.

"I'll never in the wide world be able to get that number off by Christmas," Holly observed to Craig. She had dreaded hearing his I-told-you-so when things first got out of hand, but he hadn't said a word. In fact, he had taken to dropping in evenings to help her mother pack the finished dolls and also to pot and spray golden trees, for which she was getting constant reorders. But, with the way things were going with the dolls, she wished she had never started the golden trees.

"What are you going to do about all your doll orders?" Craig wanted to know now.

"All I can do is to write post cards or letters to all but a few hundred and ask them if they can wait for after-Christmas delivery or if they want a refund."

"Isn't that sticking your neck out?" he asked in what Holly considered his usual cautious manner.

"It wouldn't be fair to have people think they could expect delivery any day and then not have the doll turn up until weeks or months after Christmas. If there's one thing I've learned, it's the obligation to fill an order as quickly as possible—by return mail if I can. I've got to let them know so they can get something else if they'd rather not wait."

"In bills and checks and money orders we have seven thousand and fifty dollars," Hugh informed her when she asked him for a financial statement. "That's a lot of money," he gloated.

"Oh, but even if we could fill all the orders, I couldn't keep anywhere near that. I clear a dollar on each doll. That would make"—she did some figuring on the back of an envelope—"fourteen hundred and ten dollars final take. But lots of people will want their money back."

"Why write them?" he asked, just as Craig had done, and she had to explain all over again.

Then the mailbox began to fill up with cancellations. Just as there had been a stampede for orders, now it was coming in reverse. With regret she turned back checks and money orders, or converted the cash she already had into money orders. It was heartbreaking to have been so near the long-awaited bonanza and then have it slip through her fingers.

Several weeks had been lost because of Duncan's failure to let her know he wasn't continuing. But, even if he hadn't disappointed her, she realized now he wouldn't have been able to cope with such a quantity of orders unless he had farmed out work. As for herself, she was lucky even to have the two sisters and their assistants.

It wasn't until well after the Christmas season—a nightmarish period of working late and starting early—that she and Hugh did the final figuring. All she had to show for the tremendous effort was what might have been a profit of four hundred and thirty-two dollars. But from this she had to deduct the cost of over a thousand postals, which ran to over twenty dollars; postage and envelopes to return checks and money orders, which totaled fifty dollars. Then there was the money she had paid the girls who had done all the addressing and stuffing—

The mail-order fiasco of the century—that was her unhappy distinction. Where she was going from here she had no idea. Right now she was too tired to care and too upset to think clearly.

The day before Christmas her father had come home from the express office with two bushel baskets of assorted citrus fruits from Duncan to the entire family. He had also sent her a small package by air mail. When she opened it on Christmas morning, she discovered an exquisitely fashioned ceramic set—a choker, a bracelet, and earrings all representing a lady's-slipper type of orchid in creamy white with delicate white markings. "This," the accompanying note read, "was designed especially for you and there will be no copies." It was signed, "Yours as always, Duncan."

[162]

Craig in turn surprised her with a most unexpected gift—
a golden brown cocker spaniel puppy with whom she and
the entire family had promptly fallen in love.

What with being at sixes and sevens about her mail-order
business and the two men in her life it was small wonder
that she was in an unhappy state of mind and completely
at sea about the future.

CHAPTER

18

HOLLY ELLIOT AND THE FAIR-CHILDS RETURN FROM MONTH'S TRIP TO FLORIDA

Looking at the headline in the *Goodhill Gazette*, Holly still found it hard to believe that she had actually made the break and had her long-awaited trip to Florida. When, in mid-January, Alice Fairchild had said "There's no reason why you can't come with us this year, Holly," her habit of staying home was by now so strong that she had automatically protested she couldn't get away. But her family had persuaded her to change her mind.

"If anyone needs a break from routine, it's you," her father had insisted.

"At your age you want to see something of the world and it isn't as though you didn't have a little money," had been her mother's comment.

It was true that the sum she had cleared on the dolls would more than take care of her trip to Florida. But it could also cancel out her indebtedness to her father and leave her with a tiny nest egg.

"Someday if you're flush and you'd like to repay me, all

right," had been her father's reaction. "But at the moment you need a change of scene."

Holly was glad she had taken their advice. The Fairchilds had been wonderful traveling companions. While Clem was busy with the citrus-plantation accounts and Alice was visiting friends, Holly took a five-day circle bus tour that started and ended in Jacksonville. Although Sarasota was included in the tour, she had resisted the impulse to look up Duncan.

Several days after Christmas she had had a long special delivery from him. He hoped she had forgiven him for not being able to do anything about the doll order. He also hoped he hadn't put her to too much inconvenience. As he was a creative artist, there was a limit to how long he could turn out a given item and, with his high standards of craftsmanship, he naturally couldn't have assistants. He had closed by saying he would call her New Year's Eve.

But he hadn't called. That wouldn't have been so bad if she hadn't turned down an invitation from Craig because of the expected phone call, saying she had a previous engagement. He had looked as though he were going to make some comment, but then he hadn't. Actually she would have welcomed a good verbal scrimmage to clear the air.

All the way home, up along the Atlantic seaboard, the thought that Craig hadn't come to see her before she left, nor even phoned, was a vivid hurt, just as it had been on the way down.

Even Lottie wasn't her usual cordial self when Holly dropped in at the shop with Goldilocks, her dog, the day after her return.

"I didn't expect to see you back," was her comment.

[165]

"Why do you say that?" asked Holly.

"Once you fell under the spell of Florida"—the implication about Duncan was unmistakable—"I didn't think you could tear yourself away. By the way, when is the wedding?"

"What wedding?" echoed Holly. "The only one I know about is yours."

"Aren't you going to marry Duncan Moore?" Lottie challenged.

Holly's eyes opened wide. "I didn't even see him while I was in Florida."

"You didn't? Then why do you treat Craig the way you do? What do you have against him?"

"I—against Craig?" Holly was too astonished to say anything else.

"Then why don't you say 'Yes' or 'No' to him?"

"You talk as though you thought he had asked me to marry him."

"Well, hasn't he?"

"No."

"Oh." Lottie seemed taken aback. "I gave him credit for being more aggressive than that. But sometimes people in love prefer uncertainty to the chance of an outright 'No.' " She looked embarrassed. "Looks as if I've played the part of the complete fool!"

"Lottie, don't talk that way!" Holly protested.

"Well, I apologize. And, after the way I've acted, I wouldn't blame if you turned me down."

"What is it you want me to do?"

"I was going to ask you to take charge of the shop while Andy and I are on our honeymoon."

"I'll be glad to look after things, Lottie."

"You're an angel."

"Don't be silly."

In the meantime Holly had some problems of her own to work out. One thing was sure—never again would she let herself or her family in for a Christmas season like the one just past. To offer something in a magazine where the readership numbered millions, you had to have something that could be turned out more quickly than dolls. Even if she had had all the necessary heads and arms and legs, she would have had to have many more people working for her. She would have had to have a large workshop or factory, as Craig had suggested. As a matter of fact, she didn't have much heart for anything now. For her mail order had always been closely connected with the idea of marriage and, at the moment, she had no particular incentive.

While she was in the doldrums, a letter came from *Hodgepodge* asking her if she would consider being the doll editor for the magazine. So many of the readers had seen her Cuddle Cutie in the grocery-store magazine and had written in about it, quite a few had also written in about seeing her Duncan Moore doll in the decorating magazine, and others who had bought her rag-doll patterns had been so pleased over them that they had written to the editors. If she would say "Yes" to the assignment, which would mean turning out a monthly column based on questions sent in by the readers, they would be very happy and they mentioned a sum. Holly wrote back to say she would be delighted to take over. It seemed wonderful to have a concrete assignment and she immediately set about doing some library research.

Now that she was concentrating on the subject of dolls, other ideas came to her. Her rag-doll patterns had been popular. Why not promote them in other magazines besides *Hodgepodge*? Better still, she could develop her patterns further by offering a Large-as-Life-Dolls series—a newborn baby, then one for each year through eight, and also a teen doll that would be around fifty inches in its finished size. All she needed was to figure out some inexpensive way of having them printed in quantity; design an envelope with drawings of the series on the front and directions for making the dolls on the back.

While she was developing this project, she had a phone call from the woman's commentator at the big television station in Hartford. She had seen the Duncan Moore doll in the home-decorating magazine, and would Miss Elliot come and appear on her program the following week to tell some of the interesting sidelights about selling things by mail? Also would she bring along as much of her work as she could easily carry?

"Anyone would think I was a success or something," Holly told her family at dinner. "Imagine asking me to appear!"

"You don't object to a little free publicity, do you?" asked her father.

"Of course not! But maybe people will get the wrong impression—think I'm prosperous or something." Right now she was down to twenty-three dollars.

"It's when people think you're doing well that they often come around with offers," her mother suggested.

Holly reached for a bunch of grapes that were part of the

fruit centerpiece. "I don't expect any business from being on the program."

"Anyhow, it's a story," put in Hugh.

"We'll print it in the *Gazette*," added Roy.

As part of her preparation for being on the television show, Holly made up one of her Large-as-Life-Dolls the same size as a little two-year-old neighbor child. This and her golden trees made a hit with the glamorous commentator and the announcer who worked with her. As soon as the program was over, a woman called and ordered a doll for her granddaughter and half a dozen golden trees. That was immediately followed by another phone call to ask if a pattern for the doll could be bought. Two days later the station forwarded a Manila envelope full of mail—more orders for golden trees and a letter from the pattern editor of a well-known pattern company which also brought out a magazine. Since she worked from her Connecticut home, the editor wrote, she had caught the show and was very much interested in the big rag doll. Would Miss Elliot like to work it out in assorted sizes? If so, in addition to a substantial royalty they would be glad to pay her for the graduated patterns.

Then Craig phoned her, the first time since she had returned from Florida.

"Lottie told me about your being on the show and I saw it. I tried to reach you at the TV station before I had to catch a plane to Washington, but the lines were busy—that's why I haven't called till now. You looked wonderful on the screen—natural as anything."

She managed a "Thank you," wondering what Lottie had told Craig.

"By the way, how's Goldilocks?" he asked.

"She's getting cuter every day. Wish I could have taken her along to Florida. I really missed the little rascal."

"I'll have to drop in and see her one of these days."

"Do that little thing."

As she turned from the telephone wondering if it was the puppy or herself he wanted to see, her mother called, "Could you put on a coat and come out in the garden?"

Thrusting above the snow were three long rows of shrubs. "Your Connecticut holly," her mother announced. "You can certainly put it on the market next Christmas."

The holly put her in mind of the catalogue she hadn't been able to get out for last Christmas. Perhaps this was the time to start lining up her other items.

"That's wonderful," she told her mother, her head already buzzing with new ideas.

Did she dare offer the Duncan Moore dolls again when there was a possibility she couldn't meet the demand in time? Then she remembered something she had read in *Hodgepodge*. People liked to make things themselves. Why not get up a doll kit with the head, arms, and legs of the Duncan Moore doll; the pattern and directions for the torso; enough unbleached muslin to make it, cotton batting to stuff it; material and patterns for the dress and lingerie? With printed directions and patterns, that would largely be a packaging problem. Then she could also get some of her local contacts to work on quick-to-make items such as the golden trees which she had dreamed up for fun and which were turning into such an unexpected business success. You never really could tell in advance what would catch on. At least she'd know enough to advertise the golden trees for next Christmas.

Lottie's wedding was to be held in Philadelphia at the home of one of her aunts. Today the Fairchilds were giving her a shower.

"I'm sorry you'll have to miss the wedding because of the shop," Lottie said. "I would have liked you to catch my bouquet."

Holly smiled ruefully, thinking, Suppose I caught it, would it make catching my man any easier? Back in December I would have said Duncan for sure, but he isn't worth Craig's little finger. Her thoughts were interrupted by the fortuneteller who was adding hilarity to the occasion.

"I see an engagement within the year," she told her. And that, Holly reflected, was pure fiction, the sort of thing that was invented to keep single girls happy at a party for a bride-to-be. Getting to be a cynical piece, aren't I, she reflected half-humorously just as Clem Fairchild ushered Craig into the hall.

"Came to do a little trucking," he commented to the assembled company with a self-conscious air.

If Craig saw her, he took no special notice. But when Clem came in alone after helping him load the car, he pantomimed to Holly that he'd like to see her. "Craig thinks some of the breakable things should be held and he wondered if you'd go along with him."

"Of course," she answered almost without thinking, and followed him to the coat closet for her wraps.

Craig seemed glad to see her. But their talk on the way

over to Woodbury and back was of generalities. It was only after she had made a second trip with him and he stopped in front of her house, which people had finally started calling the Elliot place, that he said something which might be construed as personal.

"I'm going to be gone a week or so after Lottie's wedding. I'm going to drive her to Philadelphia. When I get back, there's something I want to ask you."

The implication was unmistakable. Holly's heart beat wildly. It could only mean one thing—yet, knowing Craig, she realized he might have something else in mind, such as asking her to go into partnership raising plants; so she decided to pass it off lightly. "Lucky you're not going to be around for a while. Otherwise I'd press you into service in the shop."

After that night Holly didn't see him alone again. But as he and Lottie were pulling away from the shop, he winked at her as if in secret understanding.

Because Lottie hadn't wanted to leave the place unattended at night, Holly, Hugh, and Goldilocks were sleeping there. Just a short while before, her mother had managed to acquire a small second hand truck for plant deliveries and hauling garden supplies, and in this she brought Hugh down every afternoon shortly before dinner with a meal for the two of them ready to heat in the oven.

"Almost forgot to give you this," her brother told her one night while they were eating. He drew a slightly crumpled post card out of his pocket. It was a Florida scene and she assumed it was from Duncan, but it was signed "Craig." He hadn't mentioned where he was going or what he was doing;

and all the message said was that he'd be seeing her soon, exclamation mark.

"The guy's sweet on you, isn't he?" commented her brother.

Holly was indignant. "You didn't read it, did you?"

He reached for two of the homemade doughnuts their mother had sent along. "Sure. Why not? A post card's public property. . . . By the way, how do you feel about him?"

"That, my dear brother, is not for publication in the *Goodhill Gazette.*"

"Can't you tell me in confidence?"

"You and Roy don't even know the meaning of the word."

When the dishes were done, while Hugh was doing his homework, Holly got out the card again. It was postmarked Fort Pierce. What was Craig doing in Florida?

Later that evening, just when she was rechecking all the doors before going upstairs, the phone rang. It was long distance and the voice was Duncan's.

"My goodness, Holly, your mother gave me a start when she said you weren't home. I was afraid you were married or something. . . . How have you been?"

"Very busy."

"So have I, getting out the most wonderful new line. Wait till you see it. . . . You still put out with me about the doll?"

"No."

"You sound mad though."

"Could be."

"Why?"

"Where were you on New Year's Eve?"

"New Year's Eve." He puzzled over this. "New Year's Eve?"

"You were going to call me."

"I was? And I didn't? Well, I apologize and I'll make it up to you. But first I have the most wonderful news. I'm in New York and I'm going to be on TV in the morning—NBC. Eleven o'clock. I called so you'd be sure not to miss it. I'm showing the new line too. After I have that off my mind, let's celebrate my debut before the cameras. Do you walk without crutches now? Can you dance again?"

"I've been dancing since last fall," she informed him dryly.

"Good. Well, since that's the case, we'll cover all the swank night spots. Can you be down tomorrow in time for dinner?"

It was as though her mother were standing at her elbow. "Duncan, I can't possibly come down. If you want to see me, you can come to Connecticut."

"Well, of course if you'd rather I did . . ."

Hanging up, Holly was surprised and a little triumphant at how readily he had agreed. They had even settled on a time for his coming—Saturday night.

CHAPTER

19

The television show on which Duncan was to make his guest appearance was half-way over when the shop bell tinkled. Hurrying out, Goldilocks in her arms, Holly was startled to see Craig.

"Craig! Your post card just came yesterday! I didn't think you'd be back so soon!"

He smiled. "You know how post cards travel. How've you been?"

"Fine," she replied, then explained that she was watching for a friend to come on television and did he want to come in the den with her?

"Why not? I've got all kinds of time today," he agreed, following her.

Holly would have preferred watching Duncan by herself. With Craig in the room she felt nervous and self-conscious.

"I'll fix you coffee as soon as this is over," she told Craig, who already had the puppy on his lap.

"I'm fine just as I am," he replied with a warm smile.

At quarter of eleven, when Duncan still hadn't been introduced, Holly decided that either she had been mistaken about the time or there had been a last-minute change.

"It doesn't look as though he's going to be on," she observed to Craig.

His expression was quizzical. "I didn't realize it was a he."

Just then Duncan was introduced. He sat there perfectly relaxed, his hand on the collar of his Great Dane, impeccably dressed and wearing the charming smile she remembered so well. On a table in front of him were figurines of Seminole Indians. This must be the new line. She leaned forward to see everything and catch every word.

The minute the program was over, Craig got to his feet and put Goldilocks down. "Holly, it completely slipped my mind till now; but there's someone I have to see on business. So if you'll excuse me—"

"Can't you stop long enough for coffee?" she asked.

"Thanks, but I'm afraid not," and he left.

Holly was too stunned to speak. Hadn't he said he had all kinds of time? Instinctively she realized his departure had something to do with Duncan. But that was so childish. Or was it? Well, anyway, Duncan was coming on Saturday. But in the middle of the night Holly awoke. She had twisted and turned and tossed in her sleep and now she knew what was troubling her. *She didn't want Duncan to come up. She didn't want to see him again ever.* Granted he had surface good manners and made all the appropriate gestures, but he was a self-centered and selfish person. And as far as his work was concerned, he was a butterfly—highly artistic and talented but flitting from idea to idea without fully developing any. Unlike Craig, he just didn't know the meaning of self-discipline.

If he really knew me and what I'm thinking, he'd probably consider me horribly smug, she thought. I'm a plodder —one of those persons who make progress slowly. Even my ideas come hard. Guess that's why I want to keep using them all. But I really deserve the booby prize of the year. When I think of the casual way I've treated Craig— And when I think how wonderful he's been to me— The next time I see him I'll have to figure out some way of letting him know that, from now on, Duncan Moore is completely out of my life.

On this note Holly fell asleep again. As soon as she awoke she composed a "letter follows" telegram to Duncan. In the morning, between customers and answering the mail queries, she composed the note. It was a friendly but final message in which she told him how much she had enjoyed his television appearance. She realized, too, that since his time in New York was so limited it was expecting a lot of him to come all the way up to Connecticut for a chat with her. Also —and this was stretching the truth more than a little—she had just become engaged. In a postscript she added that she was planning to continue with the Duncan Moore dolls if he had no objection and she would automatically send him a small royalty for each doll sold.

With the letter in the mail she felt a lot easier in her mind and she looked forward to seeing Craig. Each time the shop bell tinkled or the phone rang, her heart beat just a little faster. But there was no sign from him that day or the next or the next. He was acting just as though the Wagon Wheel had a big quarantine sign on it. Sunday her mother wanted her and Hugh home for dinner, but Holly persuaded her that it would be a lark for all of them and a change, too, to cook Sunday dinner in Lottie's kitchen. What she didn't add was that if Craig should come looking for her he would be sure to find her.

By the following Sunday, after another week of complete silence from Craig, Holly was quite apathetic as to how she spent the day. When her mother mentioned that the Fairchilds had invited them all to go to the flower show in West Hartford, she decided that she would go along. Meanwhile she had had an unexpected letter from Duncan—it had been very nice of her to write; he wished her and her fiancé the very best of everything; as for royalties, he wouldn't dream of accepting any. The lavish gesture—that was Duncan all over. Craig could be honest to the point of bluntness, but even that didn't bother her now. All she minded was his silence. But there was no sense brooding during the long trip up to Hartford.

The day had been overcast, matching her mood, and now it began to rain. When they reached the Armory, where the show was being held, long lines of people, holding umbrellas, were inching their way toward the entrance. Inside, Holly caught her breath at the beauty of the gardens—the golden glory of a tulip plot, a carefully planned backyard with crocus-ringed goldfish pool, a low barbecue fireplace that continued as a stone wall sandwiched with earth where flowers grew, a lush tropical orchid plot . . . and then, miraculously, over in a corner labeled CONSERVATION, she spotted Craig.

"Let's look at the conservation exhibit," she urged her mother. If he was surprised to see her, he gave no sign; but

[178]

his manner was reserved. When the others moved on, Holly told them she would catch up with them by and by.

"I haven't had a good look at the prize winners yet," she announced to Craig, heading for the table on which there were two dioramas, or small stages, depicting a valley—one showing up wasteful practices with eroded hillsides and no grass or trees; the other with a cover of grass and trees. When she had examined them long enough to make her stay plausible, she turned to him.

"Have you made any plans for Lottie's homecoming tomorrow night?"

His tone was still diffident. "Outside of calling for them at the station in Seymour, no."

"I think we ought to do something more than that, don't you?"

"We?" The way he said that made Holly realize how deep was his hurt.

She decided to change her tactics. "Do you have to be in charge here all afternoon, Craig?"

As she spoke a blond, apple-cheeked young man came hurrying up with a breathless air. "I hope I'm not late in relieving you, Mr. Wilmot."

"Then you can walk through the exhibits with me." Before he could refuse, she tucked her arm in his and led him away. Somewhere there must be a chink in his defenses and she was determined to find it.

But, though Craig went with her, his attitude did not change. Where Holly waxed lyrical, he continued reserved.

"I think the flowers are beautiful, don't you?" she finally challenged him.

When his manner still remained glum, she decided to try a different tack. "Goldilocks misses you."

"She does?" His tone carried no conviction.

But Holly was not ready to give up. "Honestly, how some people can go for Great Danes when they could have cocker spaniels is just beyond me."

Craig looked surprised. "You mean you don't like Great Danes? I thought you were crazy about them."

"Wouldn't have one around the house if someone made me a present of one," and she gave him a mischievous smile.

"You wouldn't?" Her subtlety had not been lost on him. Slowly his grim expression gave way to a smile.

They had been walking past the prize-winning table settings featuring novel flower arrangements. Ahead was a counter where corsages and cut flowers were sold, and Craig bought her a violet corsage. At last, reflected Holly, burying her nose in the delicately fragrant flowers, she was making a little progress.

"We haven't decided what to do about Lottie and Andy," she remarked now, bringing the subject back to the newly-weds.

They had just agreed on a little dinner party—only the four of them at Lottie's house—when the Fairchilds and her mother caught up with them.

"Ready to go?" they smiled.

Holly looked at Craig.

"I'd drive you home, only I have another stint here this evening," he told her.

She didn't see him alone again until the following evening when they left Lottie's together for the drive back to

Goodhill Road. Radiant Lottie and her doting Andrew had seemed to enjoy the meal she had prepared—steak, frozen peas, French fries, tossed salad, and, to go with the ice cream, a fudge cake she had made the night before.

"You ought to be a chef," Andy had complimented her. But Craig hadn't seemed to have much of an appetite. He was still silent as they headed down the main street. But, instead of continuing south, he turned at the soldier's monument.

Holly looked at him questioningly.

"I thought we'd drive up to Bethel Rock," he explained.

Holly had been there only once before, but she knew the rock was a natural pulpit and that the first settlers had used what was now Orenaug Park for their meeting place. Whatever was troubling Craig, he would tell her up there.

After Craig had parked the car, they made their way to the pulpit in the moonlight.

"Makes you feel awfully close to the past, doesn't it?" she commented.

"Right now I'm more interested in the present."

Holly was conscious that Craig was looking at her intently. A moment later he had her in his arms.

"I've been in love with you a long time, Holly," he murmured. "Ever since that afternoon you broke your ankle. That did something to me."

"But why didn't you say something, Craig?"

"You had your mind on the gardenia bush, remember?" he reminded her half humorously.

"Oh."

As they walked back to the car, Craig's arm about her,

Holly looked up at him. "You know, Craig, I never thought I'd live to say this, but I'm really happy about the idea of living in the Housatonic Valley with you. It's home now. And, besides you, I have my family and just loads of friends—"

She could feel his arm stiffen and drop. Speechless, he looked down at her.

"Craig, what's the matter?"

"Holly, I thought you hated the valley. I thought the only way I'd stand a chance with you was to find work somewhere else. Since you seemed so crazy about Florida, I applied for a job in the conservation department there."

"Florida! Craig! Oh, no!"

Dressing for a date with Craig several evenings later, Holly tried to analyze her feelings about Florida. She remembered how she had hated the valley at first—and see how she loved it now. She realized then that she could adjust to any place. She wouldn't really lose her family or friends if she went to Florida—she would make new friends too. As for her mail-order business, she could carry that on anywhere. But, most important of all, she would be with Craig—and home was where the heart was.

Looking for a paper clip to hold together some old snapshots she wanted to show Craig, she went into Hugh's room. He usually kept his supplies in the middle desk drawer. As she bent down to open it, her gaze fell on a yellowed, slightly dog-eared sheet with a handwritten "Run Now" penciled above the typewritten story. The headline read:

HOLLY ELLIOT TO WED
WELL-KNOWN CONSERVATIONIST

How long had her brother known?

Picking up a pencil she scrawled "How right you are, Hugh!" under his notation, then hurried happily down the stairs to meet her future.

2 12 F.W.